LETTERS TO CAROLINE
Bayou Nights, Book One

BARBARA MCMAHON

Chapter One

The insistent rapping on the brass knocker added urgency to Caroline's rapid crossing of the wide foyer. Her stocking-clad feet made no sound on the cold expanse of marble. She ignored the discomfort. Her heart felt just as cold. She thought the last mourner had departed only moments ago. Had they forgotten something?

She was tired—too tired to deal with much more. The entire last six weeks had been emotionally draining. Today's funeral had been the final straw. She thought she'd melt in the unseasonably warm February sun. Louisiana was supposed to cool down a bit in winter. Of course, nothing else had gone right over the last few weeks, why should she have expected anything different today?

She longed to crawl into bed and forget everything at least for the night!

Opening the door, she tried for a semblance of a smile. Only to have her efforts freeze when she saw the last person on the face of the earth she expected to see—Brandon Madison.

A tidal wave of emotions surged through her. Disbelief, anger, sorrow and hurt combined with a hint of disbelieving joy. She stared at her husband, unable to say a word.

Whatever was he doing here? Or were her eyes playing tricks on her? Was she losing her mind?

After ignoring her for five years was he truly standing on the doorstep large as life and twice as sexy?

"Hello, Caroline," he said in a voice she'd never forgotten. "Going somewhere?"

He looked at her black dress, the single strand of pearls, the neatly sleeked-back hair, then the bare feet. His glance gave nothing away. He'd always been good at not letting his emotions show.

Slowly her gaze mimicked his and traced over him from his dark conservatively cut hair to the tips of his shiny wing tips as if she sought to imprint every detail on her mind. He looked older, of course. And harder, like tempered steel.

She had an eye for fabric and style—his suit looked as if it'd cost more than her monthly rent and his shoes almost as much. He looked toned, healthy and as successful as he'd always yearned to be.

Success, she remembered instantly, had been vitally important to him. Obviously he'd attained what he wanted.

But at what cost?

For a moment a sharp pain in her heart almost buckled her knees. She gripped the doorknob tighter, depending on it as if it were a lifeline. It'd been half a decade since their brief seven-month marriage ended.

If someone had asked her yesterday, she'd have sworn she was long over Brandon Madison. She'd put him and their life together behind her and moved on. She liked her life now and wouldn't go back even if she could.

Her unexpected feelings at seeing him disproved that.

She glared at him. What they had was over long ago. Yet, one look at the man and old feelings began to resurface.

The primary ones being hurt and betrayal—and an overwhelming sadness from the death of a dream.

"This is a surprise, Brandon. What are you doing here?" she asked as he continued to stand on the wide veranda. She wanted to slam the door in his face as if that would slam a lid on the churning memories that bubbled up.

Proper behavior, drilled into her from infancy, kept her from acting so rudely.

"I came to see you."

The even tone in his voice was nothing like the hot passionate tone he'd used in the dark of night when it had been the two of them against the world.

Before he'd let her down.

Before he'd ignored her, blamed her, turned from her to make work the most important focus of his life—even more important than his own wife.

"I don't want to see you."

It sounded childish. She didn't care—she only wanted him gone. Hadn't she endured enough past and present to get a bit of a break?

"You've made that perfectly clear over the years. It's time to—"

"Who is it, Caroline?" Michelle entered the foyer from the living room.

She, too, was dressed in black. Her high heels clicked on the marble floor. "Well, I declare. Brandon!"

She stopped and stared at the man in surprise. "We didn't expect you."

"Michelle."

He nodded briefly in acknowledgment, his eyes taking in the difference between the sisters and the similarities. Caroline was older by eighteen months, but several inches shorter than her slender younger sister. Both had deep blue eyes, but Caroline's hair was a dark brown while Michelle's was a rich deep auburn.

"What're you doing here?" Michelle asked, glancing between her sister and Brandon. If she sensed the tension, she gave no sign.

Caroline started to turn, wondering if her knees would support her if she let go of the door. Wishing she dare slam it shut, bolt it and pretend she'd never seen the man, she refrained. Old lessons were hard to ignore.

She so didn't need this today of all days!

"I asked him the same thing. Apparently he's here to see me," she said irritated. She'd thought the worst was over, that there'd be some peace at last. Was she never to have a moment's serenity again?

Michelle smiled in polite welcome. "We didn't expect you, Brandon. How did you hear?"

Brandon glanced from one sister to the other, narrowing his eyes in assessment. Suddenly things began to add up. He hadn't risen as swiftly as he had in business by ignoring obvious clues.

He looked at Caroline. "A death in the family?"

She nodded. "Grandmother."

"I didn't know."

Brandon had come to see Caroline, to resolve the issue they'd ignored for five years. Their marriage was over and it was time to formally end it. He had the divorce papers in his pocket not trusting the mail since she had a habit of returning letters unopened.

Normally his timing was perfect. Apparently not today.

"That explains your opening the door," he said. "Eugenia would never have let that menial task be performed by a member of her illustrious family." Bitter animosity colored his words. He never liked Caroline's grandmother.

"I don't need your sarcasm. Grandmother's help was given the week off. Of course I opened the door."

"We're the only ones here. Come in," Michelle said. "No sense letting all the cool air escape. It's hot as Hades outside. Early February and it feels like July! I thought I'd melt at the cemetery."

Brandon glanced at Caroline—raising an eyebrow he waited for her to speak. He was startled to find her looking so pale and thin.

What had she been doing over the last five years? Besides ignoring his attempts to get in touch with her?

For a moment, he felt a hint of concern. Ruthlessly damping down on the unexpected feeling, he reminded himself why he'd come. What they had ended. She was no longer his concern.

She'd had endless opportunities to contact him, to respond to his attempts to reach her. Her refusal to deal with him, made her position crystal clear and relieved him of any guilt at the way things turned out.

Once she signed the papers, once the divorce went through, he need never see her again.

"Come in, then," she said reluctantly. "I can't imagine why you chose today to show up."

"When did Eugenia die?" Brandon asked stepping inside and pushing the door closed behind him.

Caroline released the knob before she came in contact with Brandon, glad to see her knees worked. Only, with the door shut, the foyer seemed to shrink. Taking a step back to put some distance between them, she frowned as she studied him.

She didn't want Brandon here. She didn't want to see him. She didn't need any more emotional turmoil. And especially didn't want to feel the mixed feelings his presence unleashed. There was enough on her plate now with her grandmother's death and her ramblings before she died. Caroline didn't need anything more to deal with.

"She died Thursday night. We just came from the funeral a little while ago. You missed the wake," Michelle said. "Half the town was here. Some were grandmother's friends, others I think just wanted to crash the party to see the house."

"What are y'all doing out here?" Abby Talmadge stopped in the doorway and looked at the group. Her face lit with delight when she spotted Brandon. Spontaneously she dashed across the floor and flung her arms around his neck exuberantly.

"Brandon! What a surprise! How wonderful!"

Almost as tall as Michelle, Abby looked totally unlike either of her two older sisters. Her ash-blond hair seemed at odds with the darker shades of her sisters'. But her smile was pure Talmadge, along with her deep blue eyes.

Caroline watched, wishing she dare yank her younger sister away and send her to her room. Abby had always had a warm spot in her heart for Brandon. Five years ago at seventeen, she'd considered him totally romantic. Even now, after all that had transpired, she obviously continued to harbor warm feelings for him.

Traitor, Caroline thought. Then felt stricken. It wasn't her sister's fault she liked Brandon. Abby didn't know the entire story. Her heart hadn't been broken, her life left in tatters.

And whose fault was it that she didn't know, a voice inside asked. Caroline never told the full story to anyone but her grandmother.

Had things been different, had Brandon followed her, contacted her years ago——?

No! She refused to even think along those lines. He hadn't. End of that story. She'd moved on. She has a great career, friends. That chapter of her past was behind her.

Except—for a split second Caroline wished she could feel the warmth of his arms holding her, could lean against his hard body, draw on his strength. Just once more. She was so tired.

And she felt so alone. There were decisions to be made and she wasn't entirely sure how to proceed. Should she tell her sisters the revelation her grandmother had rambled on about or look into it to see if there was any truth to the matter?

"So did you come to help settle the estate?" Abby asked excitedly. "We've missed you, haven't we?" Her gaze swept the others in the foyer. Her bright smile hard to resist.

"No." Caroline said quickly, glaring at Brandon. "There's no need for you to be here. We've managed without you for years. We can certainly manage another death in the family without your help."

Abby looked stunned at the harsh tone.

Michelle blinked, her watchful gaze moving back and forth between her sister and Brandon.

No one ever mentioned that. Not in all the years since Caroline returned home.

The tightening in Brandon's jaw was the only sign he heard. His expression gave no hint what he thought.

"I came to talk to you. The timing may be inconvenient, but I'm not leaving until you and I sit down and talk."

Something held back the scathing words he'd planned to say once he saw Caroline face-to-face. He'd had years to refine them, until they conveyed exactly his contempt for her actions. Granted, he hadn't behaved admirably under the circumstances himself. But her behavior had been inexcusable.

Seeing her again, realizing her grandmother had died, he held back. Even he had some sensibilities—though he was sure she'd disagree. Time enough when things settled down a little to attend to business. If she thought he'd give up now that he was here, she didn't know him. He'd stay until he got her signatures on the documents.

He wouldn't return to New Orleans until he had her

signature. But he wouldn't insist on her doing anything today with her grandmother so newly deceased.

If needed, he'd stay a couple of days—keep in touch with the office via phone. It wasn't as if he made a habit of being away.

Now that he was face-to-face with his wife for the first time in five years, he was taking no chances. They'd settle the matter before he left, inconvenient time or not!

"I'd say the timing's inconvenient. I still can't imagine why you drove all this way. What do you want? Why today? Why not just call?"

Caroline yearned to open the door in a sweeping gesture and usher him out. She knew she couldn't force him to do anything he didn't want. She'd never been capable of that.

No one was. When Brandon got a notion he could be the most stubborn man alive.

"We're going to talk. Instead of futile attempts to reach you by phone, I came in person," he said. "If I'd known about your grandmother, I'd have waited a couple of days. But I didn't know. We can either talk now or in a day or two. I'm not leaving until we get some things settled."

"Everything was settled years ago. Seems to me, anyway."

She knew she sounded petulant, but she couldn't help it. Seeing him brought old memories to the forefront. She didn't like it one bit. One more thing to deal with and she was so tired she just wanted to sleep!

Instead she felt drawn to him. Being near him stirred her curiosity and anger. She wanted to rail at him for leaving. She wanted to discover what he'd been doing for the last five years.

How she wished she could change the past! That had been her mantra for those first few months five years ago.

"Running away never solved anything, Caroline," he said.

"Maybe Abby and I should wait in the living room," Michelle said.

"No need. I have nothing to discuss with Brandon. Sorry you made the trip for nothing."

Caroline turned and almost ran up the stairs, escape uppermost in her mind. So what if he thought she was running away. It was too late to dream dreams with Brandon at the center.

Truth be told, she'd been operating on sheer nervous energy for days and she'd explode if she didn't get away. This was too much. First her grandmother's illness; then her unexpected death; now Brandon's reappearance after hearing nothing from him for five years.

It felt as if the world was crashing down on her. She could use a little help not have more problems thrown her way. Would she be capable of administering the probate and managing the estate until the inheritance was settled? Her home was in Dallas, not Baton Rouge. She'd never had to deal with anything like this before.

And how could she cope with the myriad of problems, if her whole being became caught up in the old memories or endless recriminations and regrets tied to Brandon?

The man she'd loved more than life itself.

The man who'd abandoned her at the worst moment in

her life. First she'd lost their unborn baby then her husband.

The man she sometimes feared she still loved, despite all that had passed between them and the years that separated them.

No, no, no, she murmured as she hurried down the long hallway.

She refused to let herself be caught up with that reckless emotion of love. It hurt too much when it ended.

Picking up the pieces of her shattered life hadn't been easy. But she'd managed. She'd built a successful life for herself in Dallas. So what if she didn't experience the joyful delights she'd once found with Brandon. Neither did she have the depths of bitter pain and betrayal to contend with, either.

Except with the startling revelation from her grandmother right before she'd died.

It couldn't be true, could it? Even Eugenia Talmadge couldn't have been that self-serving, that vindictive, that manipulative. That wicked!

That strange tale had been the ramblings of a delirious, dying woman, that's all. Caroline tried to convince herself it was that and nothing more.

She closed her bedroom door and flung herself on her bed. The room was dim. Out of habit, she'd closed the drapes earlier to keep the hot sun from fading the carpet and heating the room. Now she wrapped herself in the light coverlet and closed her eyes. Fatigue gripped her. She longed for the oblivion of sleep, but Brandon's face danced before her eyes.

Why had he come? How soon would he leave?
Slowly sleep claimed her.

Brandon watched Caroline flee up the stairs. For a moment he almost pursued her, fed up with her refusal to talk with him. Nothing had changed. She avoided him at every turn. Just as she had so long ago.

Only this time he wouldn't be put off.

His attorneys could have had the papers delivered. Brandon hadn't wanted to risk it. She'd returned his letters before. This time he'd make sure she couldn't do that. He admitted his own curiosity and need for closure had him decide to deliver the papers in person.

Only he hadn't expected Eugenia's death. Somehow he'd thought the woman would live forever.

For a moment he wondered what Caroline would do without her formidable grandmother to hide behind.

"Come in and sit down, Brandon," Michelle said, looking after her sister with worry in her eyes. "I'm sure she'll be back soon. It's been a stressful few days."

"Longer than that for Caroline," Abby said leading the way into the living
room. "She's the one who came home to care for Grandmother when we learned she was so ill."

"Was Eugenia sick for long?"

"Several weeks," Abby said. "And it's still taken its toll. She looks exhausted."

"Tell us what you've been doing, Brandon. We haven't seen you in years."

"It has been a while," Brandon acknowledged as he followed the two sisters into the huge formal living room.

Quickly he noted the elegant furnishings, the paintings by the famous artists on the wall. Nothing had altered since he'd last been in this room. It still felt as cold and impersonal as a hotel lobby or a museum. It was a perfect setting for Eugenia Talmadge. Ornate, luxurious, pretentious. At least in his mind.

Baton Rouge was full of antebellum homes. Many were in various state of disrepair or had been turned over to an historical trust. Only a few of the old mansions were still owned privately.

Eugenia Talmadge had gripped hers tightly with both hands, changing nothing in the home that'd been in her husband's family for generations. She'd taken inordinate, arrogant pride in every stick of furniture, every painting, every piece of silver. She'd never let up on the heritage of the Talmadges compared to the last of such from the boy from the bayou.

He'd once longed for such a setting—costly furniture, valuable paintings. To make it big to show her he could provide for Caroline as Eugenia wanted.

Only discovering once achieved that it offered cold comfort.

While the house remained the same, Caroline's younger sisters had changed. Michelle was tall and slender and lovely. She'd been nineteen when he last saw her. Still living under Eugenia Talmadge's domineering thumb, shy and studious. He wondered what she was doing now.

Did the sisters all still live in the old family home? Or had they, like Caroline at that age, broken away and tried to make a life away from Talmadge Hall?

Abby offered him some punch from the amount remaining in the silver bowl on the buffet against the wall and sat beside him on the brocade sofa. The remains of the recent wake were evident throughout the room with cups and glasses and empty plates everywhere.

Abby had changed the most, he mused, sipping the small glass she'd brought. A high school senior when his marriage ended, she'd blossomed into a beautiful woman, bright and sassy if the trend of her conversation was any indication. Had she stopped talking since they'd sat down?

"—so of course I had to come home, just like you, Brandon. Family rallies around in the time of crisis, right? It wasn't easy getting time off. We are always swamped. But then, hospitals are always shorthanded and the number of patients seems to increase every year."

"Abby, you're babbling. Shut up and let Brandon get a word in edgewise," Michelle said with a smile, sitting on the chair near the sofa. She didn't appear as open and friendly as her younger sister, Brandon noted. From loyalty to Caroline? Or her own innate reserve?

"I'm interested in what she has to say," he replied.

It always paid to discover what he could about the people he'd be dealing with. His years growing his business proved that. These women had the closest ties to Caroline. He'd learn more about her through them.

"Do you both still live here?" he asked.

Michelle shook her head. "Actually Abby and I live in New Orleans. We have for several years."

"Moved out as soon as we were old enough to escape," Abby said irrepressibly.

He raised an eyebrow in surprise. "You've been in New Orleans all this time? You should have called me."

Michelle looked at him gravely. "I didn't think you wanted any more involvement with the Talmadges," she said. "And it's not as if we move in the same circles, is it? We've seen how successful Domino Software has become."

"Still, as Abby says, we're family."

Until he got Caroline's signature on the papers he carried—until the final link was severed.

Then he frowned. Why had he said that. Eugenia Talmadges had never considered him part of the family. She'd done her best to stop Caroline marrying him and then criticized him at every turn.

He hadn't thought a minute about family ties when Caroline left. Angry at her decision, he'd been determined to prove to the world, and to himself, that he needed no one. His parents never understood his goals. The new family he tried to forge had come to a tragic end; going alone had been the one option he followed these days.

Abby took a sip of punch and studied Brandon. "We missed you," she said.

If he were honest, he'd admit to missing them. Missing Caroline most of all, but also her adoring sisters. He was an only child. He'd enjoyed watching the sisters interact during the short months of his marriage. Had been almost envious of their closeness.

"Where do you two live?"

"I live in a great apartment not far from the downtown area. Abby has a place in Metairie. She works at St. Joseph's Hospital," Michelle replied.

"And Caroline?" He had to ask. Curiosity was a burning desire to know more about her even as he was about to cut her totally from his life.

"She has a condo in Dallas. She never goes to New Orleans. She never comes to visit us," Abby said.

The sudden silence proved awkward. Each knew why Caroline never returned to New Orleans, though no one said it aloud. The memories were too painful.

"You'll plan to stay here, won't you?" Abby invited to break the tension. "There're a dozen bedrooms upstairs. And it'd be so nice to have you right on the spot to help out. Being in business you must have a better idea than we do of what to expect in winding down the estate and how to handle things. We don't have a clue. And I hate the thought of Caroline coping with it all on her own—look how thin she is and how tired. Since she's the eldest, Grandmother designated her as executrix. Now I'm worried about her."

"I hadn't planned to stay at all," Brandon said, setting his glass on a coaster on the Queen Anne table. From the dirty glasses, cups and plates stacked haphazardly here and there, he guessed the place had been full of people only a short time before he arrived. Thank goodness he'd been late enough to miss that!

"Oh, do stay. It'll be weeks before the estate gets put into probate and then months for it to go through the entire process. Caroline will probably have a dozen questions. We've never gone through this before. Stay just a day or so," Abby said, leaning close, her eyes beseeching.

"If you can manage it, Brandon, please do. Just to make sure Caroline has a handle on things. I can only be here until tomorrow. I hate the thought of leaving her alone to deal with all this, but I can't get any more time off from work right now. I'll come back on the weekends. But it'd mean a lot to know she has someone here with her," Michelle added.

"And I have to be back on duty tomorrow night. Michelle and I are driving back together tomorrow. Do stay at least another day, Brandon," Abby urged.

"I hardly think Caroline would appreciate such an arrangement."

Surprised, he actually considered it. He'd never liked Eugenia Talmadge, but she'd been Caroline's grandmother. The woman who had raised the girls. Caroline had loved her, and her death must be a huge loss. An empty house would be hard to deal with.

Maybe he'd stay over. He'd once loved Caroline. He'd never thought they'd come to this. Would it hurt anything to stay another day?

Silence filled the bedroom when Caroline awoke. Turning on her bedside lamp, she looked at the clock. It was after eight. Slowly she stretched, still feeling tired, overwhelmed. Life had been simpler two months ago, before her grandmother had become so ill, before Caroline's world had been turned upside down a second time.

Changing from her black dress to a light cotton robe, Caroline fastened the buttons pensively. She was starving—not surprising when she considered how little she'd eaten recently. Had Brandon left already?

Hurrying down the stairs, she listened for voices. Where were Michelle and Abby? The living room was tidy once again. Obviously they'd cleaned up the mess. Had they gone out to dinner?

Pushing open the door into the kitchen, Caroline stopped in surprise. Brandon looked up from the open refrigerator and caught her eye, letting his gaze travel over the robe. He straightened slowly and closed the door.

"I thought you'd be long gone by now," Caroline said.

For one confusing moment, she wished she'd brushed her hair, freshened her makeup. Pushing the thought aside, she tried to figure out why he was still here.

And how to slow the rapid increase in her heart rate. She refused to let herself be attracted to him again, just because he looked wonderful. Ruthlessly ignoring her clamoring senses, she tried to remain cool.

"Not yet. Your sisters are changing their clothes, then we're planning dinner. I thought I'd look around and see what we might find to eat in here. Otherwise, we'll go out. What happened to your grandmother's cook?"

"I gave her the week off. She was quite upset. She was devoted to Eugenia."

"Mmm." He leaned against the counter, crossing his arms over his chest.

Caroline noticed he'd discarded his suit jacket somewhere along the way. His tie was loosened at the neck, the collar button unfastened. He'd rolled up his sleeves over muscular arms. He looked at ease, at home.

And suddenly fascinating.

She remembered being held in those strong arms. Being kissed—

She looked away, trying to forget the stubborn memories.

"Some people liked my grandmother," she said defensively, hearing the skepticism in his tone. Brandon had never been one of them.

"Hungry?" he asked, deliberately changing the subject.

Caroline hesitated. While she didn't mind hunting up some soup or sandwich fixings, she hadn't expected to share a meal with Brandon. And especially not cook him one. On the other hand, if he took her sisters to dinner, she'd spend the evening alone. She didn't want to miss time with Abby and Michelle—their visit was too short as it was.

"Caroline, it's a straightforward question. Are you hungry? You look as if you're considering some major life change," he said impatiently.

"I already had that." The words came unbidden. Horrified, she stared at him in dismay.

He drew a deep breath. "That's what I've come to discuss."

Shaking her head, Caroline stepped back bumping against the swinging door. "No. Not now. It's far too late to change anything by talk, Brandon. If you and my sisters want, I can prepare something for dinner."

"Or we could order something, have it delivered."

"Oops," Abby said as she pushed against the door and barged into Caroline. Peering around the corner, she stepped into the kitchen once her sister moved.

"I see you're up. Are you hungry? We thought we'd go out for dinner, unless you found something, Brandon?"

"Nothing that wouldn't take a long time to prepare. I was telling Caroline that we could order in."

"Oh, that's sounds great. Does that Chinese place on Royal Street still deliver?" Abby asked Caroline.

"Yes, I think so."

If she didn't look directly at him, maybe she could ignore him, ignore the emotions that were all mixed up. Maybe she could pretend he was merely an acquaintance.

Letting Abby carry the conversation, Caroline tried to concentrate, but her thoughts were churning too much to pay strict attention.

Until Abby said something she couldn't possibly believe.

"What did you say?" Caroline asked, her startled eyes meeting her sister's.

Abby looked at her, smiling brightly. "Just that Michelle and I are pleased Brandon agreed to stay to help you during the next few days. We feel terrible leaving you with all the work. And we didn't like the thought of your remaining here all alone."

Horrified, Caroline turned to look at Brandon.

His gaze met hers and her heart sank. The amused gleam in his eyes did not auger well for her immediate future.

Chapter Two

Caroline stared at him in disbelief. "You aren't staying here!"

"He can help," Abby said.

"I don't need help," Caroline protested.

Brandon stared at her, trying to ignore the clamor of his senses, the heightened awareness being near her brought. Even with her hair mussed and dark circles beneath her eyes, she was beautiful. Too thin, yet with an allure that still had the power to captivate. He instantly evaluated his options. He could find his jacket, pull out the papers and insist she sign them, then and there. Take that final step to end their marriage for once and for all. That'd remove him from her proximity which she seemed to want.

He could have it out with her once and for all. Let her know how her leaving affected him. Tell her how disgusted he'd been when she'd chosen her grandmother over him.

But something held him back.

She looked too fragile—as if she were at the end of her rope. For all he knew she'd be glad to sign, glad to get him out of her life. She'd made her position clear years ago.

He hadn't succeeded by ignoring his instincts.

"I've said I'll stay a couple of days. If you don't need my help with the estate, then I'll be gone—after we have our talk."

And after she signed those papers.

Caroline stared at him mutinously, her eyes narrowed in anger. She brushed a hand through her hair.

Brandon clenched one hand to keep from reaching out to touch those silky tresses. His fingertips remembered the soft texture. Did she still smell of lilacs? Taking a deep breath, he imagined he could detect the scent from where he stood.

Caroline raised her chin, obviously frustrated by the turn of events. He almost smiled at the familiar gesture as bittersweet memories surfaced.

"The time for us to talk was five years ago. There's nothing left to say. But if you don't mind wasting your time hanging around here, do what you want."

"I don't think it'll be a waste of time," Brandon said as he studied her. "If nothing else, we'll clear things between us. But after Abby and Michelle leave. I don't wish to air our dirty laundry before all and sundry."

"Since you're here for dinner, I'll go change," she muttered.

Leaving the kitchen with her head held high, Caroline hurried to her room. She sat on the edge of the bed. Why had he shown up now? What was so important he wanted to talk to her today? Why not six months ago or six months in the future? Or five years ago when she needed him so much?

Slowly she rose to change into casual clothes. She wondered if she could get Brandon alone tonight and find out what was so important. What was there left to say? The past couldn't be altered. They'd each moved on. She had a good life in Dallas that suited her. She knew he'd succeeded beyond what either of them expected when they were first married.

Pulling on a loose cotton dress, she slipped her feet into sandals and went back downstairs.

Michelle and Abby were chatting easily with Brandon when Caroline entered the living room.

"We ordered Chinese," Michelle said. "It'll be here soon. Want something to drink?"

Caroline motioned Michelle to stay seated. "I'll get some iced tea."

A quick glance at Brandon showed him firmly ensconced in the chair near the sofa, his long legs stretched out before him, his right hand casually holding a tall glass. For a moment her heart threatened to stop, then skipped a beat and began to pound.

When he looked at her with those familiar dark eyes, she felt the heat rise in her cheeks. One look and she spun back to that shy college freshman who had been so enamored with the young computer techie who'd singled her out and courted her so assiduously.

Not that he was that much older than she, only five years. He'd been twenty-five when they married. He was thirty-one now. But when he'd been courting, he'd seemed so much more mature than she felt.

Turning away she knew she needed to get control of her emotions. She needed to somehow ignore the pull of attraction that rose despite her best efforts at keeping a distance.

Brandon was not for her. That had been made clear five years ago.

"Brandon's been telling us about his software company," Michelle said.

Caroline sat gingerly on a chair opposite Brandon, hoping her sisters wouldn't comment on how far the seat was from the rest of them.

"Your software company?" she asked. She'd heard from her grandmother when he'd first started up. The older woman had scoffed at his efforts, saying firms in California did more for the software industry than any in the south—especially New Orleans. She'd been so critical.

Thinking back, she realized that was Eugenia's strong point—criticizing every thing and every one. It had been hard trying to please her when growing up.

Caroline studied her glass of tea, wondering if she dare ask how he'd started his own company. He'd often talked when they were first married of his plans for developing business-changing software. Dreams of making it big.

She wasn't surprised to learn he'd succeeded. But he must have devoted every waking minute to achieve so much in only five years.

Would a show of curiosity on her part be misconstrued as interest? Would he read more into a casual inquiry than was warranted? She couldn't help being curious. Each time a memory would surface over the years, she'd ruthlessly squash it. She was over him!

Dreams had been another thing. Something she couldn't control. How many times had she dreamed his arms were around her again, his deep voice speaking softly in her ear.

What else had he been doing since she'd last seen him? Or had business consumed him to the exclusion of anything else?

Work had consumed him to the exclusion of everything else when she'd lost the baby. Did he forget about people and other commitments in his quest to make more money? Was he still striving to get ahead and become even more rich and powerful? Or had things changed at all since she left?

"How long before the food arrives?" she asked. She refused to be drawn into his life again. Once was enough.

Brandon's teeth gleamed white against his tan as he smiled directly at her. "Changing the subject, Caroline, or just trying to ignore that I'm here?"

She glared at him. "That's hard to do when you take up so much space."

He raised an eyebrow sardonically. "One small chair?"

He seemed to dominate the room. She felt his presence where she sat. A quick glance at her sisters surprised her. Didn't they feel that magnetism, the power? Was she alone affected?

Michelle and Abby were comfortable on the sofa, Abby with her feet on the coffee table. Eugenia would have had a fit to see that.

They looked at her. Michelle's expression was

speculative. Abby grinned.

"It's nice to have a man around. This house was too long just women."

"He's not staying," Caroline murmured, annoyed her sisters didn't seem to see anything awkward or wrong about Brandon's being here.

When the food finally arrived, Caroline insisted they eat in the dining room, though her sisters had opted for the more informal kitchen table. Caroline didn't want informality or a semblance of coziness with Brandon. She needed to keep him at a distance to keep her own emotions under control.

Even with the length of the table between them, however, she was aware of his every move. Of how he cut his egg roll. Of the way his throat moved when he swallowed, the way his hands held the teacup, the way his hot gaze focused on her more often than she wanted.

The meal seemed endless and Caroline thought she'd go crazy.

When they finished, Abby and Michelle insisted on doing the few dishes they'd used.

Caroline faced Brandon. "We could talk now," she said, certain she wouldn't sleep a wink if she didn't discover why he'd come.

"Not tonight, Caroline. You look exhausted. Why not get a good night's sleep first?" Brandon said gently.

Great—he thought she looked awful. Not the words a woman wanted to hear. Especially from a man she'd like to show she'd managed fine without.

Abby popped back into the dining room and wiped up the table. "Am I interrupting?"

Caroline shook her head and rose. "Not at all."

She'd have argued with Brandon, but he was right, she was too tired to even think straight.

"I'm going up to bed."

"Good idea," Brandon said, his dark eyes mocking.

"Are you all right?" Abby asked.

"I'll be fine once I get some rest."

And once she got away from Brandon.

She prayed Eugenia's estate would be clear-cut and easy to deal with. If there was no need for Brandon's help, he could leave tomorrow when her sisters left.

After they had that talk he wanted. Was he going to ask for a divorce? Had he found someone else?

She felt numb. It was long past time to make a decision, to release their bond and let them each continue their lives.

Yet somehow she'd never thought about divorce.

She wasn't sure she wanted one. Yet why not? They hadn't lived together for five years. She'd made a new life for herself in Dallas. He'd obviously succeeded in New Orleans. Maybe he'd leave in the morning.

She needed time alone to close up the house and search through her grandmother's papers to see if she could discover anything at all surrounding her father's disappearance. She did not need to deal with Brandon at the same time.

As Caroline prepared for bed, she forced her thoughts away from her estranged husband and tried to remember as much as she could about her father. He'd married her mother for her money and when it wasn't forthcoming, he left. That is, if the teachings of a lifetime could be believed. It was what they'd been told by their grandmother who blamed him for her only daughter's death.

But Eugenia Talmadge's delirious words during her final weeks raised strong doubts in Caroline's mind.

Caroline grew up believing her father deserted her mother, broke her heart and caused her depression which resulted in an early death. Eugenia insisted that when she refused to settle any money on him, he'd turned his back on his children, his responsibilities, and had taken off for greener pastures. His wife and family hadn't been enough to hold him.

But was that the whole story?

Was it even a semblance of the truth?

She wished she'd tried to get more information from her grandmother. But the fever that raged had her delirious much of that time, and when the fever was gone, she refused to talk at all.

After Caroline left Brandon excused himself and went out onto the wide veranda. The sultry night air felt good after the sterile coolness inside the house.

He walked to the edge and gazed over the dark lawn. He'd have to call the office first thing tomorrow and inform his assistant he wouldn't be in on Monday. Reviewing the meetings he had on his calendar, he'd also have her reschedule a few. He could make calls from here.

They hadn't stayed often at the old home. Eugenia had done all she could to make it an unwelcoming place when Caroline married against her wishes. He let his mind wander. He was surprised to realize once he'd seen her he'd wanted Caroline again. Irrational, he knew. And lately everything he did had a logic that made for no wasted emotion, no wrong moves. For years he'd tried to put her out of his mind. Sometimes even succeeding for a few weeks at a time.

Then he'd see someone who reminded him of her. Or catch a hint of the perfume she used to wear or hear a song she loved. Defying logic, memories would flood to the surface.

Sometimes he'd dream about her.

It was past time to cut the tie, to get her out of his life and move on.

Yet seeing her raised familiar longings. What was there about Caroline that captivated him? That caused a ruthless, logical businessman to postpone a confrontation and stay when she so clearly didn't want him? Had she missed him at all these last years? Did she ever regret the way things played out?

Caroline slept in late the next morning. Once awake, she felt refreshed for the first time since she'd come home. Dressing quickly, she went to find her sisters. They were in the kitchen already preparing lunch. Feeling extraneous, she leaned against the counter and chatted with them while Michelle prepared a shrimp salad, a fruit salad and a plate of cold cuts.

Abby set the table and called Brandon.

Scarcely greeting Brandon, Caroline sat and hoped she could eat with the butterflies in her stomach.

Michelle looked at Abby and Caroline and then spoke,

"Caroline, I'm sorry to leave you with all the work regarding the estate, but if it makes it any easier, I for one never plan to live in this house again and vote we sell it."

Surprised, Brandon looked at Caroline. "I thought this was your family home. Hasn't it been in your family for generations?"

She nodded.

"Do you want to sell?" he asked.

For a moment Caroline thought about it. She hadn't looked beyond discovering what she could about her father's disappearance. Michelle's idea had merit.

"Might as well. I don't live here."

There were few happy memories, more of those of a bitter old woman who cherished prestige and power and money and didn't care who she stepped on to get it.

"Me, neither," Abby said firmly. "I couldn't wait to escape when I graduated from high school. Sell the blasted thing. We can split the money and Michelle and I can buy something more suitable for our current life-styles. I love New Orleans. With my share from the sale, maybe I could buy a condo or something like you did in Dallas."

Brandon looked up at that. "How long have you lived in Dallas? I thought you lived here with Eugenia," he said slowly.

"Almost five years," she said.

"What do you do there?"

She could tell this was all news to him. Not that she expected him to keep up with her after she left. If he'd ever gotten in touch with her, he'd have known of the changes she made to cope.

"I work in real estate." She said briefly. She looked at her sisters.

"We'd need to go through everything so I know what to keep and what to get rid of before we put the house up for sale. Once we clear out any clutter, we can stage the place to show best, then collect any furniture we want after the sale," Caroline said slowly, already dreading the monumental task of sorting through several generations of accumulated furniture, clothes and memorabilia before they could put the place up for sale.

"Goodness, what an undertaking. I'll come up on weekends," Michelle said. "This is our busiest time or I'd ask for more vacation days."

"I'll come up on my days off," Abby added. "And see if I can swap some time with other nurses."

Caroline nodded. "I'll get started and y'all come and help when you can."

Abby and Michelle looked at Brandon. "Maybe you could lend a hand," Abby said brightly.

Brandon nodded, his gaze fixed on Caroline. "I'll stay for a couple of days."

"You don't have to stay at all!" she snapped.

Brandon shrugged. "I'll stay another day or two in case

you need some muscle. And maybe learn more about Dallas. I thought you were living with Eugenia—having tea with the garden club or giving a tour at one of the historic homes."

Abby and Michelle looked from one to the other. "She didn't want to stay here anymore than we did. You know what grandmother was like," Abby said.

Brandon nodded, his expression thoughtful.

The two sisters planned to leave shortly after lunch.

Once packed, Michelle sought Caroline. She found her sister in the study going through some of the papers on the desk.

"Are you feeling all right?" she asked, closing the door softly behind her. Crossing to sit on the edge of the desk, she looked closely at her sister.

"I'm tired. It's been an exhausting few weeks. And Brandon's unexpected reappearance hasn't helped. I'll be fine in a day or two."

"Brandon looks good," Michelle said, playing with the letter opener.

"No matchmaking," Caroline warned. "I won't be drawn in again."

Michelle shrugged and glanced around the room. "It was a long time ago, sis. People change. Men never say much, but maybe he came because he wants another chance."

"I doubt it." But for an instant a flicker of hope glimmered. Could that be the reason for Brandon's visit?

"Why else would he show up?"

"I have no idea...he's scarcely said two words to me." She didn't want to tell her she thought it might be about a divorce. If so, why was he offering to stay?

"Give him a break. He hasn't had a moment alone with you since he arrived."

Caroline kept silent. She wondered why Brandon had really come. Was he trying to make amends? Had he changed?

It didn't matter. The chasm was too large. If she couldn't depend on her husband in a time of crisis, she'd rather go it alone.

"He'll be gone in a day or so and things will go on," Caroline said slowly. Closing her eyes, she wondered if she would ever regain her strength, ever feel full of energy again.

"It's odd to know Grandmother's gone. She was such a strong force in our lives," Michelle said, idly tracing patterns with the letter opener.

"Too strong," Caroline said. "She wasn't happy unless she could run things—even our lives. She practically forced me to date that friend of hers, Thomas Sinclair, and he's years older than I. She kept harping on what a wonderful alliance that would be."

"Is that why you never divorced—to make sure you couldn't be persuaded into an alliance?" Michelle asked unexpectedly, looking directly at Caroline.

"Alliance. Isn't that dynastic? I never thought about it before, but do you suppose that's what she and grandfather had—an alliance instead of a happy marriage?" Caroline asked, deliberately sidestepping her sister's personal question.

She wished she knew for sure the reason Brandon had come.

"I don't know. She sure was taken with the Talmadge name. It always seemed as if she thought it deserves some kind of monument or something. And she just married into it. It wasn't as if she'd been born into the family. She wasn't really a Talmadge."

Caroline looked at her sister. "We aren't really Talmadges, either, you know."

Michelle looked puzzled for a moment. "Oh, yes, you're right. I almost forgot."

"Eugenia was Mama's mother. But when Mama married our father, she took his last name. She obviously took the Talmadge name back after the divorce and changed ours to match."

"Because she was so angry at our father she didn't want us to use his name, do you suppose?"

Caroline shrugged, longing to tell her sister what Eugenia had muttered over and over.

Suddenly she had more questions than she could count.

What had happened twenty-three years ago? Had their father really abandoned them as they'd always been told? And if so where was he now? Was there any way to find out the truth? Searching for answers had to come second to getting the house ready for sale. But she'd be on the lookout for anything that might give her a clue.

Caroline saw her sisters off later that afternoon, remaining on the veranda after the taillights disappeared down the long driveway. Even in the shade, the afternoon felt oppressive. Conscious of Brandon standing a few feet away, watching her, she shivered despite the heat and crossed her arms across her chest. If he didn't stop watching her every move, he'd drive her crazy!

Taking a deep breath, she turned and looked at him, tilting her chin, drawing on years of training under the eagle eye of Eugenia Talmadge.

"You can leave now as well," she said politely, the edge of frustration coloring her tone.

Slowly he smiled, amusement dancing in his eyes as he stood leaning against one of the support pillars, his arms across his broad chest, his shirtsleeves rolled up. He had to be hot in the late afternoon sun, but he looked cool and controlled.

"I don't think so, Caroline. We have some unfinished business between us and now's as good a time as any to get it resolved, wouldn't you say?"

"Is that why you came? To talk about the past?"

"Why I came isn't as important as why I'm staying."

"And why is that?"

"I told you, to get things resolved."

"Seems to me we resolved things five years ago."

"Really?" He stepped forward, his arms dropping to his sides. "And I said running away never solved anything. Did you ever think about me after you left, Caroline?"

Before she could even think of a response, he lowered his head and covered her mouth with his.

Shocked, Caroline felt the past and present merge until she had no idea where she was.

Brandon's lips moved against hers as passionately as ever, as familiar as her own heartbeat. For a long moment the world stood still. Every cell in Caroline's body recognized Brandon's touch, his taste, his scent. His fingers threaded into her hair as he cradled her head in his strong hands. The world spun and Caroline almost forgot the years that had separated them. Almost forgot the painful past and the tragedy that had ripped their world apart.

She couldn't think, couldn't remember, could only feel. Feel the spiraling sensations that danced throughout her. Feel the glorious heat that warmed her soul. Feel the past and present swirl together until there was only timeless floating.

Endless eons later, Brandon raised his face, his eyes narrowed as he took in her bemused expression. When his features hardened, she drew back, realizing instantly what she'd allowed. What she'd participated in. What she'd enjoyed.

"I didn't leave you, Brandon. I left an empty apartment." She bit out the words, and whirled, walking swiftly toward the front door.

Confusion gripped her. How could she have responded so fervently? She should have pulled back at the first sign he wanted to kiss her. But she hadn't expected it.

And once he touched her she'd been lost.

He swung around and called after her, "You don't have your grandmother to run to this time, Caroline. There's just you and me here now."

She paused by the door and stiffened. "And pretty soon there'll only be me, Brandon. You won't stay. I don't seem to have much luck with men staying in my life, do I?"

"What men?" His voice was sharp.

She turned to look at him. "First my father, then you. Isn't that enough?"

"If you are comparing me to your father, maybe you should also compare yourself with your mother. What part did she play in driving him away?"

"What do you mean?"

"I still remember your telling me how you felt by his abandoning you and your sisters when you were a child. But maybe part of the fault lay with your mother. Maybe you and I were only repeating history—maybe she left him."

"Actually," Caroline began slowly, the urge to share her discovery too strong to resist. "I'm not sure he did leave. Voluntarily, that is."

"What do you mean?"

She hesitated. "I guess it can't hurt to tell you." She gazed over the wide expanse of lawn gathering her thoughts. "Something my grandmother said before she died makes me wonder if my father left of his own volition or was driven away. She made it sound as if she'd something to do with his leaving. She forced him to go."

"How could he have been driven away by Eugenia?"

"I don't know. That's what I plan to find out. All my life I've thought it was something I did that made him leave. Maybe he didn't want little girls, what if he wanted sons instead. Or maybe I was too bratty."

"For heaven's sake, you were four when he left. You couldn't have done anything to drive a man away."

She nodded. "Rationally, as an adult, I know that. I think

I know that. But we're talking about a child growing up. My mother was dead, my father gone. Kids take on responsibility when there's none there. He could have left because of me, because he didn't want to be tied down with a child."

"Highly unlikely. If he hadn't wanted a child, they would have stopped at one, not had two more—although if you were only four at the time, I assume he wouldn't even have known about your mother being pregnant with Abby."

She shrugged. "I don't know much about it, but I plan to find out. If there is anything in Grandmother's papers, I'll find it."

"What are you expecting, some sort of journal in which she confesses all?" he asked.

Caroline lifted her chin. "That's unlikely, I know. Yet there might be something somewhere. I said it wouldn't be easy. But knowing the truth might make a world of difference to me. Especially if I find out he didn't deliberately abandoned me—us."

"What do Michelle and Abby think about this?"

"I didn't tell them. There's the possibility that Eugenia was merely delirious and didn't know what she was saying. Maybe she was hallucinating. I don't know. The first time she said she'd fixed it so he had to leave, I really thought that's what it was a delusion. But she repeated it over and over, so I began to think maybe it wasn't just rambling, but the past coming alive for her."

"And if you don't find anything?" he asked.

"If I can't find anything in her papers, I'll look farther afield, see if anyone in town remembers that far back."

"You should hire a private detective to find out."

She shook her head, smiling in embarrassment. "It's not that big a deal. I don't need to find the man, just discover if he left or if Eugenia drove him away. It's been twenty-three years. If he hasn't tried to contact us after all this time, I guess he doesn't want to see me or my sisters. But I'd like to know what really happened back then."

"It won't change things. He'll still be gone."

"It could change how I feel about him," she said slowly. "All my life I've felt abandoned. Maybe I wasn't."

"You realize it is probably a futile effort?" he asked.

She nodded.

Against all logic, he spoke, "I'll help you look, as long as I'm here."

Brandon wondered why he kept postponing his departure. It had nothing to do with how she felt when he kissed her. Nothing to do with the passion he felt in her. He wasn't even sure why he'd given in to impulse to kiss her, except she'd been standing there and he hadn't been able to resist.

It changed nothing.

They'd had seven glorious months together. When their happiness ended with her miscarriage, she'd packed and left.

He wouldn't leave himself open to such desolation again. Once he obtained the divorce, he had no immediate plans to remarry. In the morning, he'd give her the papers.

Or, he could stay through the weekend. Today was Thursday, it'd only be three more days until Monday. He could stay and help Caroline look through her grandmother's papers to see if the old woman had indeed been instrumental in driving away her father.

Stay and prove to himself that he was over her.

"Why would she do such a thing?" he asked a minute later, considering the different ramifications.

"I don't know. I know she wanted my mother to marry into an old Louisiana family. Instead, she ran off with my father. They settled here at Grandmother's insistence, I think."

Caroline refused to give voice to the hurtful words her grandmother always said, calling her father a no-good, worthless drifter. A child didn't need to hear that about her own father. But her grandmother hadn't been big on psychology for children and forged her own ruthless path.

"Let's get started," he said, heading for the door.

Surprised, Caroline looked at him. "I thought you wanted to talk."

"Later."

"I don't want you to stay," she said desperately as he stepped closer.

"And I didn't want you to leave five years ago. Looks like we don't always get what we want. Where do you want to start with Eugenia's papers?"

Caroline flung open the door and hastened through before Brandon could get too close. Why had he agreed to help her? Distrustful, she glanced at him, keeping her distance.

"I'll take the help," she said carefully, "but no more kisses."

She didn't care if she gave herself away, it was too dangerous to have him think he could kiss her whenever he wanted. She wasn't sure she could withstand temptation.

He smiled sardonically and deliberately took a threatening step closer. "No promises, Caroline. For someone who says she doesn't want any more kisses, you sure responded as if you did."

"I don't want to discuss it!"

"Running away again?" he asked softly.

She shook her head and walked calmly through the foyer to a door at the far end, her heart racing. She'd never admit it, but running seemed the most prudent plan right now!

"Eugenia used this as her study and office. Any papers she had would most likely be in here."

Brandon stepped into the doorway and looked around.

"It shouldn't take too long to go through this." There was a small desk, one old oak file cabinet and several shelves of books. "However, I doubt you'll find anything from twenty years ago here. There's not enough room to store records for that many years. Would she have put earlier years elsewhere?" he asked.

"In the attic, I suppose. It covers the entire width of the house. We were never allowed up there to play when we were children. I don't think I've been up there more than a half-dozen times in my whole life."

"Interesting possibility. Let's eliminate this first, then we'll check that out."

Caroline glanced at her watch. "It'll be dinnertime soon. Rosalie isn't due back until tomorrow. Want me to fix us sandwiches or something?"

"We could order in a pizza," he said, already opening the top drawer of the polished desk.

For a moment another time flashed before her eyes. Ordering pizza had been their one extravagance when they'd been married. One they indulged in as frequently as their budget would allow. Memories bubbled up, splashed over. She hugged herself and looked around. She hadn't had a pizza in years.

Yet, it obviously meant nothing to Brandon. Unaware he'd said anything disturbing, he withdrew a stack of papers and began to sort them.

Shaking off her melancholy, Caroline went to the phone and dialed. She had to put things into perspective. They were married, yet had lived apart for far longer than they'd lived together. They had their own lives now. And no room for memories of their time together.

In fact, she was somewhat surprised Brandon had never filed for divorce. She knew why she hadn't, but why hadn't he? She opened her mouth to ask him, and snapped it shut.

Her life was in enough turmoil right now, the last thing she needed was further discussion on why their marriage ended. And when to finalize the demise.

Maybe once she learned about her father, she could move on. And if that meant legally ending their marriage, she'd definitely consider it.

But what if Brandon didn't want to end it, a small voice whispered. What if he had hopes she'd return? What if his kiss had been to prove to her they still belonged together?

Nonsense! It was time to forget the past and concentrate on the future—and see if she could discover the truth about her father.

Why had that thought even crept up? When she'd needed him most after losing the baby, he'd been conspicuously missing. She'd left and he hadn't tried to contact her, hadn't followed to bring her home.

If he'd cared at all, he'd at least phoned her.

"Pizza will be here in a half hour. What are you doing?" she said, placing the phone receiver back in its cradle.

"I'm sorting business papers from personal correspondence or anything that looks like it might be personal," he said, not even looking up.

Caroline pulled a drawer from the desk and took it to a chair placing it on her lap as she sat. Soon only the sound of ruffling paper filled the room.

Once she had an idea how long it would take to clear out the house, she'd prepare it for the sale. In a few weeks, a couple of months at the most, the albatross would be gone and she'd have nothing tying her to Baton Rouge.

For a moment, she wondered if she should consider moving to New Orleans to be near Abby and Michelle. But the familiar ache vetoed that idea. She wasn't sure she'd ever want to return to the Crescent City. New Orleans was where she and Brandon had lived. And where their unborn baby had died.

The memories were too painful. There were some things she couldn't do.

When the pizza arrived, Caroline brought the box, plates

and napkins into the study. Brandon stood, scooped up two pieces and headed for the door. "I'll be back," he said cryptically and kept walking.

Caroline nibbled at a slice, wondering where he was going. She heard his car, then silence.

At least it made eating easier. She was too aware of the man whenever he was near. Too aware of the potent feelings that continued to dance along her nerves.

She should be focusing on her quest, searching for an answer.

Instead she'd watched Brandon as he quickly scanned papers and placed them in different piles. His dark hair had fallen across his forehead in disarray as he'd run his fingers through it in the course of the afternoon. She'd longed to brush it back. Longed to ask him what he'd been doing for the last five years.

And to ask if he ever thought about her.

Chapter Three

Daydreams aren't worth the paper they're written on, Eugenia had often said. Caroline could hear her grandmother's voice echoing on the night breeze. And daydreams about Brandon sweeping her off her feet and demanding that she return to him were as worthless as any. She must still be tired to permit such foolishness, Caroline thought.

It was fully dark by the time Brandon returned. Caroline watched from the wicker rocking chair on the veranda. The temperature had dropped a few degrees with the setting sun. A light breeze blew from the river, cooling things even more. She'd skimmed as many papers as she could find in the study until her eyes had become bleary.

Seeking solace, she'd come to sit in the dark on the veranda where she could smell the lingering scent of sweet jasmine and hear the gentle murmur from the Mississippi River.

And allow her imagination free rein—just this once.

She watched as Brandon pulled up before the house and got out, reaching back inside the car for numerous bags and packages and a slim briefcase. He started for the door.

Caroline knew the moment he saw her—he was almost even with her.

"I thought you'd left," she said.

He walked over and sank down on a matching rocker beside her, placing the bags and packages on the veranda.

"I didn't come prepared to stay. I had one clean shirt in the car, but if we're going to be plowing through dusty boxes in your attic, I wanted something more casual than an Armani suit."

She nodded, noting the quiet pride when he mentioned his suit.

He'd succeeded, just as he'd always wanted. Did it make him happy she wondered. Did he ever think about what they'd started building together? Their apartment had been tiny, but she'd done her best to make it cozy for them. They rarely could afford to eat out—which was why pizza was considered a treat back then.

Did you ever think about me after you left? he'd asked.

She could have answered his question a thousand times over. Which still wouldn't have conveyed how often she'd thought about him. She'd thought about him endlessly when she'd first returned home. Remembered every day they'd spent together. She'd expected him to come to get her, to demand she return, to insist her place was with him, that he couldn't live without her. She'd expected him to prove to her that he loved her far more than business. And once the initial hurt had faded, that they could build a future together.

But there'd been nothing. No calls, no letters, no visits.

She suspected that he'd been secretly relieved to be able

to discard his wife so easily. Didn't men want children to carry on? And she hadn't been able to provide that.

"I'm sorry," she said in a low voice, the old pain surging to the forefront.

"For what? I volunteered to stay. At least through the weekend."

"For losing our baby," she whispered. "I know you blamed me."

"What?" He sounded shocked. "Caroline, I never blamed you for losing the baby."

"It's all right, you know. I blame myself," she said.

"No. Oh, honey, miscarriages happen. If anything—I blamed myself. If we hadn't had to live in that apartment where you had to walk up two flights of stairs every day, maybe you wouldn't have lost the baby. If I'd been a better husband, I could have provided better for you, for the baby."

"Don't say that. It's not true. Exercise is good for pregnant women. It wasn't your fault."

Caroline was stunned at Brandon's words. He'd blamed himself?

"It sure felt as if it were my fault at the time. But as the years have passed, I wonder if there is any fault? Things like that happen. They're tragic, but not always avoidable. Can you look at any one thing and say it caused the miscarriage?"

She shook her head, blinking against sudden tears. She was through crying. She'd cried a river's worth over the years.

Yet the old pain never went completely away. She would always long for her precious baby.

His admission that he'd blamed himself, that he didn't

hold her responsible, eased the horrible guilt she felt.

Maybe, it was the way things were meant to be. She'd loved him deeply, longed to have his children, to build a loving and happy family with Brandon. And failed.

She looked over at him though he was hard to see in the darkness. His silhouette stood out against the soft illumination spilling from the windows. Her heart skipped a beat and began to pound. Surreptitiously rubbing her damp palms against her skirt, she cleared her throat. It was easier to talk to him in the dark. It always had been.

"I want to say that I appreciate your staying after all. Truth to tell, I wasn't too excited about being here by myself tonight. I don't believe I've ever stayed in the house alone. Grandmother was always here. And she usually had servants who lived in as well. It's only in recent years that she made do with dailies."

Brandon gazed out over the dark lawn, relaxing in the rocker. In the distance, he could see the glimmer of a light from the neighbor's house. The nearest neighbors weren't close. Caroline would have been all alone if he hadn't remained. Yet her admission caught him by surprise.

"Brandon?" she said.

"Yes?" Even her voice sounded achingly familiar in the dark. She'd loved to talk once they were in bed. She said the cloak of darkness made it easier to share her thoughts and feelings. He remembered he'd shared more with her than anyone else in his life.

In the end, it hadn't been enough.

"I thought about you after I left." She gave a ghost of a

laugh. "It's dumb, but I really thought you'd come after me and tell me to come ho—back."

"Sorry I wasn't fast enough," he said tightly, reaching down to gather his bags and briefcase. "I'll take these in. Did you finish reviewing the papers in the study?"

"What do you mean, not fast enough?" she asked.

"Nothing. What about the papers?"

"I glanced at them. Nothing at all about my parents. I'll check in her bedroom in the morning and see if there's anything there. After that, we can tackle the attic."

"Good night, then."

"Didn't you want to talk to me? Abby and Michelle are gone."

He hesitated, then shook his head. "Not tonight. I need to call my secretary and find out what's happened during the last two days at the office."

"Of course, business always comes first. Don't let me keep you."

Caroline sat on the veranda until quite late. The monotonous creak of the rocker soothed her. She and Brandon hadn't said much, but more had been revealed this evening than during all the weeks after the loss of their precious baby. She placed her hand over her stomach as if she could still feel that small presence. She'd miscarried in the fourth month. Just a week or two after she'd first felt the flutter of life. One terrifying afternoon, she'd lost their future.

Brandon rushed to her side from work and at first seemed as devastated as she felt.

But by the next day, he was back at work, staying longer than ever before. Even going into the office on the weekends.

When she needed love and comfort the most, he closed himself off from her—finding his own solace in work. Or maybe he'd always found that special something with his job and turned to it when times got rough.

Shivering slightly in the warm night, Caroline decided it was Brandon's presence that caused the old memories to flood. Memories made bittersweet with the passage of years.

Why was he still here? If he was staying from some misguided sense of responsibility, she'd quickly absolve him of the need. And if in the search they discovered her father hadn't left of his own volition, it might reaffirm her faith in men. Maybe.

What would reaffirm her faith in Brandon?

When Caroline entered the kitchen the next morning, her grandmother's longtime cook, Rosalie, was back—singing a gospel hymn at the top of her voice as she scrambled eggs. Brandon stood near the back door, sipping a cup of coffee as he gazed over the shaggy yard. He hadn't heard her enter over Rosalie's singing and Caroline took a moment to study him.

The pullover shirt he wore displayed his chest and shoulders to advantage. Broader and more muscular than she remembered, she wondered if he worked out or if her memory was just faulty. Though how she could have forgotten something like that, she couldn't imagine. His hair fell across his forehead and she once again experienced that longing to brush it back, to tangle her fingers in its thickness, re-familiarize herself with its texture.

Blinking she shook her head, forcing herself to think of the day ahead. The light khaki pants he'd bought wouldn't stay clean long in the dusty attic. She wondered if he'd considered that.

Her own shorts were old, the sleeveless top long past its prime. Both were perfect for the unseasonably hot weather and rummaging around dusty boxes.

"Good morning, Miss Caroline. You sleep all right?" Rosalie spotted her and turned her beaming face toward her. "Mr. Brandon's breakfast is ready and I can make your eggs however you want. Plenty of bacon and sausage, biscuits, grits and coffee. You want some orange juice?"

Brandon turned and looked at Caroline, studying her with his dark eyes. Face-to-face, Caroline realized more than his body had changed. There was no welcome in his expression, no special smile, especially for her. He might as well be a stranger.

The pang that hit her was unexpected.

"Just toast and coffee, please," Caroline said, ignoring the hint of disappointment at his lack of greeting. What'd she expected? She wasn't exactly thrilled to be stuck with him either, given the circumstances. Yet she was grateful to have someone to help her search.

Brandon stepped into the kitchen and raised his cup. "Excellent coffee, but you need more than that and toast for heavy investigating. Rosalie prepared a feast."

"There looks to be enough food for a small army,"

Caroline said, smiling at the cook.

"Nothing like cooking for the gentlemen. They have a hearty appetite and appreciation for good food," Rosalie said as she made shooing motions. "Y'all get into the dining room. I'll bring in everything. You want your eggs poached, Miss Caroline?"

"So much for listening to me," Caroline muttered as she turned to lead the way to the dining room. Brandon was right on her heels. He caught the door behind him.

"It won't hurt you to eat a good breakfast. We don't want your energy flagging."

Caroline raised her chin and turned to respond and almost bumped into him. She hadn't realized he was so close. Brandon reached out a hand to steady her, his fingers warm as they closed on her bare arm. Swallowing hard she tried to ignore the sensations that exploded from his touch. But that proved impossible. Clearing her throat, she looked up at him.

"Toast would have given me enough energy."

"For everything?" he asked slowly, his thumb making random patterns on the soft skin of her inner arm. Caroline couldn't think.

Nodding she tried to pull free. His grip tightened. Without looking away, he placed his cup on the table and reached for her with his other hand. Caroline gazed into his eyes, mesmerized as his dark gaze seemed to glow with hidden fires. Slowly she felt herself drawn closer.

Before she could say a word in protest, he pulled her against him and encircled her with his arms. Lowering his head, he kissed her again.

Caroline stood rock still for a split second before responding to his kiss. Her arms encircled his waist and she hugged him tightly. His scent filled her senses and she tried to find a rational thought that'd help end the madness.

They hadn't seen each other in years. Yet in all that time, she'd never found anyone who came close to fostering the feelings this man could with a single look.

She should remember he didn't want her. Somehow that didn't seem important with his mouth moving against hers, with his hand tracing patterns across her back, with his heart thumping heavily against hers.

"Excuse me," Rosalie said coming from the kitchen with her arms laden with plates. "You two can carry on like that later. Now you sit yourselves down and eat this breakfast while it's still hot."

She placed the plates on the table—Brandon's at the head, Caroline's to his right. Fussing with silverware and napkins, she looked over at them.

Caroline pulled away, breathing hard, her lips warm and slightly swollen. Her heart raced. For a second, she'd forgotten everything but joy.

Only—it was an illusion.

Blinking, she stared at Rosalie and met the woman's knowing gaze. Flushed with embarrassment, she pulled out her chair.

"Thank you, Rosalie, it looks delicious," Caroline said, trying to recover a semblance of normalcy. She couldn't believe Brandon had kissed her again. And kissed her like he was never going to let her go.

Nor could she believe how she'd responded. How she wanted more and actually resented Rosalie's interruption. She should be grateful for the woman's entrance. Kissing Brandon did not play into her plans for the future.

She took a bite of poached egg, aware of Brandon drawing his own chair and sitting close to her. His leg brushed hers as he settled in.

Her gaze flew to him. He smiled at her as if nothing earth-shattering had happened.

Caroline tried to eat, but the food had little taste. Her blood pumped through her veins, her breath catching. Why had he kissed her? Twice! He showed up unexpectedly and—what? Offered to help, to stay for a few days. Why?

Brandon poured another cup of coffee, raising his eyebrows in silent question to Caroline. She nodded and pushed her cup closer to him.

"Tell me about your work," Brandon said as he filled her cup. Setting down the coffee carafe, he began to spread butter on a biscuit then began to eat with obvious enjoyment.

Warily, Caroline studied him. "Why?"

Shrugging, he replied, "I'm curious. I'd have thought the garden club, Junior League and hospital charities would've kept you too busy to work."

She stiffened at his sardonic tone. Tilting her chin slightly, she glared at him. "My grandmother may have belonged to those organizations, but I don't. Of course I work. How do you think I've earned my living?"

"I have no idea. I thought you ran home to resume your

former life-style."

"I didn't come home because of that," she said. Was that what he'd truly been thinking all these years? Surely he'd known her better than that. How could he have thought—

"Come on, Caroline, you know you missed this."

He waved his hand around the elegant dining room, with the beautiful old cherry wood furnishings, the ornate crystal chandelier suspended from the tall ceiling, the fine china and elegant Revere silver coffee service.

"Our apartment was a far cry from luxurious."

She shook her head. "You're crazy, Brandon. I left because I was devastated at the loss of the baby. And there was no one to comfort me, to stand by me."

Not that her grandmother had, either. She'd dismissed the miscarriage as a trivial incident, one that allowed Caroline to resume her proper life without problems. She'd predicted Brandon wouldn't come after her and in that she'd be right.

"And you received comfort from that old woman?" he asked incredulously.

Slowly, she shook her head. "No."

"So why stay away?"

"I told you, I didn't think you cared. Besides, I had Michelle and Abby. They rallied around. Both of them were still here back then."

"You thought I didn't care because I didn't immediately come after you? Give me a break here, Caroline. I had commitments."

Pushing aside her plate, she took her cup and rose. "I was a commitment. You married me, remember? And proceeded to ignore me when I needed you most. All for work."

"Caroline. I had other—"

"I don't want to hear it! This conversation's pointless. What happened, happened. It's over. I'm going up to Eugenia's bedroom to see if there're any papers there. I called grandmother's attorney and got the name of a reputable appraiser, who will be by later today to appraise the furnishings. If you want to stay to help, fine. Otherwise, maybe you should head back to New Orleans."

Caroline left on shaky legs. Any talk of the past disturbed her. Was she ever to get closure? She'd been ecstatically happy with Brandon until she'd lost their baby. The weeks that followed had been a nightmare. Longing for comfort, for companionship, his absence had been worse than anything. His being here now made a mockery of her feelings.

She needed to find some distance.

Brandon finished the meal Rosalie had prepared, though he'd lost his appetite. He'd like nothing better than to return to New Orleans today. It made no sense staying any longer. They couldn't even eat a meal together in harmony. Nor have any kind of discussion. Not with Caroline's running away at every turn. Had he truly expected anything different from her?

Once finished with breakfast, Brandon headed for the attic. He found stacks of labeled boxes and chose two from two dozen years ago. He carried them down and dumped them on the floor in the empty bedroom closest to the attic steps.

Caroline followed him in eyeing him warily. If she could keep the conversation off the past, she might be able to relax.

Brandon glanced up as she walked in.

"This is probably a wild-goose chase, you know," he said as he ripped off the tape of the first box. "Eugenia could have been talking nonsense, Caroline."

"I know that's a possibility. Still, I need to verify it either way if possible."

"You could be opening a can of worms."

"How do you figure that?" she asked as she peered into the box and reached for a handful of paper.

He sat beside her. Close enough for him to reach out and touch her if he were so inclined.

It was a huge room, with twelve-foot-high ceilings and two sets of French doors that were open to the upper balcony. The bed didn't begin to take up the major floor space, nor did the chair, table and bureau. He hadn't needed to sit so close to her, but figured it'd make any sharing of papers easier.

"What if you learn something you wish you hadn't?" he asked.

"Like what?"

"I don't know. What if your grandmother didn't chase your father away. What if he turns out to have been the no-good drifter she called him? How'll you deal with that?"

"That's not new. I expect I'd go on like I always have. But what if he didn't leave of his own free will, don't I deserve to know that?" she asked.

Taking a deep breath, Caroline tried to calm her emotions. Instead, she caught a whiff of Brandon's aftershave. Her heart skipped a beat in memory. Shyly, she glanced at him from beneath her lashes. He concentrated on the contents of the box, allowing her all the time in the world to study him.

Which wouldn't be enough, she realized as the minutes drifted by. She could stare at him forever.

Taking another breath, she turned her attention to the papers in hand. The jumble took her aback. She'd have thought her grandmother would have been meticulous in storage. It looked as if she just dumped in every paper relating to a particular year. Sighing, she began to scan the top sheet.

Brandon stretched over and snagged a wastebasket. "Dump the trash in here. And nothing's worth keeping, unless it has some value today."

Scanning each sheet briefly, Caroline either tossed it into the wastebasket or placed it in a stack beside her.

But before long, she found her mind wandering. She skimmed over each document, but her attention focused on Brandon. She could see him from the corner of her eye. And for a moment the years seemed to melt away. It was as if they'd never parted. Wistfully she wished things had been different.

Of course, she'd wished for years that she'd had her

baby. That they could have built a family full of love and laughter.

Would Brandon have been more attentive if the baby had been born, or would he have become so consumed with making it in the business world he'd neglect his family?

If she'd had her baby to fill her days, would she have felt so neglected while he worked?

Had their marriage been doomed from the beginning?

He looked up as if reading her mind. "Well?" he asked.

"Well what?"

"What are you doing?"

"Nothing, just thinking," she said uneasily.

"About?" He looked at her curiously.

"Nothing," she repeated, too afraid to broach the subject. That way lay heartache.

"Thinking about nothing gives you that funny look on your face?"

"I don't have a funny look. Did you find anything?"

"I'm not looking, I'm talking with you. For the first time in five years, I might add."

She tilted her chin and faced him. "And whose fault is that?"

"Yours."

"If you are referring to my returning here, I wonder how long it took for you to realize I wasn't at the apartment? I mean, did you notice right away or was it several days later, when the laundry hadn't been done or groceries bought? You were never home long enough to notice I was missing otherwise."

"Not so. I knew the first night. The apartment was

empty, echoing like a tomb."

"Don't."

The memory threatened to overwhelm her. She blinked back sudden tears. Five years and she still ached. How long would it take to get over the loss. To totally get over it and move on?

"Denying it or ignoring it won't get anything resolved, Caroline. You can't hide from what happened. We both made mistakes. It's up to us to correct them if we can. And if we can't, then it's time to cut our losses and move on."

She studied the carpet pattern, wishing she were elsewhere. After the strain of her grandmother's illness and death, to have to confront Brandon was too much. She longed to stop the words, to have him stay another day or two before bringing up the past.

"You're five years too late," she said softly.

He drew a deep breath. "In more ways than one, I guess."

Glancing up at him, she frowned. "What do you mean?"

"You and I never should have married. Our worlds were too far apart."

Caroline stared at him, tears shimmering in her eyes. She didn't want it to be true. She'd loved him so much!

"When we hit our first bad patch, instead of drawing together to fend against the world, we went our separate ways. Did you think I wasn't upset about losing the baby? I wanted our baby, Caroline! It was a part of both of us."

He hesitated a moment, then slowly added, "I hated losing it for another reason. My father had been diagnosed with cancer. He didn't have long to live. I wanted him to see my son or daughter. Wanted him to have the chance to hold his grandchild, once, before he died."

"I didn't know," she whispered.

The hurt grew with each word he spoke, with each memory he exposed. She hadn't known about his father. That made their loss all the worse.

"No, you didn't know. I'd only found out a week or so before we lost the baby and hadn't talked about it. I was still trying to come to terms with the news. It doesn't matter, now. The apartment wasn't as fancy as this place, but if you'd stayed around, the money eventually came in."

"It was never about money!"

She rose up to her knees and dashed away the tears that threatened to spill over.

"It was about needing someone there for me. You were gone, I was alone day and night. Do you have any idea how difficult that was for me? We hadn't lived there long enough for me to make many friends. At least here I had my sisters, long time friends, familiar places. A time to recover while I wasn't alone!"

Brandon looked away, frowning. " I felt totally helpless. There was nothing I could do to make things right. So if I buried myself in work, it took my mind off—"

"And I needed something, too, Brandon. Only I had nothing! I didn't have a job. Nothing to consume me, so I wouldn't feel the loss every single minute. Just an empty apartment, an empty nursery, an empty spot on your side of the bed. So, yeah, I came home. You're right, obviously we shouldn't have married. I expected more than you gave me. I needed more."

His hard gaze clashed with hers. "And I expected more, as well. Loyalty and commitment."

"Don't talk to me about commitment. You were so far gone in your work that you didn't have time for anyone!"

"It was the only way I knew to cope with the tragedy."

"And what about me?" she almost screamed.

He was silent for so long, Caroline thought he wouldn't respond. Her breathing slowed, her flare of anger began to fade. Finally, he spoke.

"I let you down in more ways than I thought," he said slowly.

Deflated at his capitulation, she sank back on her heels, at a loss for what to say next.

He admitted he'd let her down? She should have felt vindicated. Instead, she only felt a huge sense of loss. She'd loved him, believed he loved her. And their marriage hadn't stood the first test.

"It's over, then, isn't it?" she said slowly. "No more hoping you'll show up one day, no more wanting to turn back the clock, make things different."

"Honey, you can't make things different. You had no control over the miscarriage. I didn't know how to comfort you. I couldn't find comfort for myself. Maybe your returning home was the best thing for you."

Standing, Caroline dusted her hands and looked at him. "The best thing for me would have been to have my husband contact me five years ago."

With that, she turned and left the room.

Chapter Four

B randon watched her leave, anger simmering just below the surface. She still had the power to infuriate him!

"It's a two way street, Caroline. You could have met me half way," he called after her.

He rose and took two steps toward the door, intent on following her. Then his cell phone rang. Reaching into his pocket, he withdrew the slim device. He growled into it.

"Madison."

"Whoa, boss. Don't snap my head off. Am I interrupting something important?" His secretary's familiar voice came through.

"No. What's up?" Betty Jean wouldn't call if it weren't important.

"We received a fax from Bendix. You said to let you know when it arrived. Do you have a fax machine there?"

"Send it to the laptop. If I don't have wifi here, I'll use my hotspot. What does he say?" Brandon asked as he began walking toward the bedroom he was using.

In seconds, Caroline's abrupt departure was forgotten, as he concentrated on a crucial situation for a customer. Setting up his laptop, he noted his suit jacket slung over a chair back—the divorce papers still in the inside pocket.

Why not just give the blasted papers to her and have done with it?

It was over an hour later before Brandon finished dealing with the myriad of details related to the Bendix situation.

That done, he went in search of Caroline. Surprised, he found her back in the bedroom where he'd deposited the boxes. By the looks of the overflowing wastebasket and stack of papers beside her knees, he could see she'd been at it for some time.

She glanced at him, immediately returning her attention to the sheet of stationery she held, saying nothing.

Brandon sat beside her and reached for another stack of papers. He'd cooled down while working through the Bendix mess. Now, despite all that had transpired between them, he was determined to discover more about Caroline before leaving.

What had she been doing over the last five years?

"You never told me about Dallas," he said a few minutes later.

She looked up in surprise. "I have a good friend there from high school. She invited me for a visit after I lost the baby. She's in real estate and got me interested. I'm my own boss. And I'm doing pretty well. Dallas is an exciting city. I like living there."

She gazed into space for a moment as if considering what else to say.

"I bet you're a success," he murmured, tossing a stack of

papers into the trash and reaching for more. "You always found it easy to talk to people. Wouldn't that be an asset in selling homes?"

She cocked her head to one side and looked at him with some surprise. "It was scary at first. I had no business experience. My major in college was fine arts—which I never finished, as you know."

"I thought you might have gone back to college."

"No."

She looked back at the papers in her hand not wanting him to know how listless she'd felt for those first few months. She'd had no energy, no enthusiasm. Just making it through the day had been almost more than she could manage. College had been the farthest thing from her mind. Jody's invitation had been listlessly accepted. But once there, she'd made an effort to be a good guest and things improved from that.

"I expect you're also a success because of your determination," Brandon said, frowning as he tossed another small stack of papers into the trash. "With your background you could suggest how people would furnish their new houses and make it a home. Have them see the possibilities through your eyes."

Caroline felt a touch of warmth at his unexpected compliment. "The homes I sell are a far cry from our apartment. You don't still live there, do you?"

He looked at her. "No. It was too empty after you left. I have a place overlooking the river. And even though I had a professional decorator furnish it, it's not as warm and welcoming as our place was. You really made it a home."

"That's nice of you to say, Brandon. I never knew," Caroline said sadly.

She wished that she'd known he felt that way when they'd been together. She'd tried so hard to make their apartment a refuge for them. She'd loved it herself, but never realized how he felt about it.

"Where do you live now?" she asked softly, a remembered fondness for the place sweeping through her. It had been her first home. Her condo now didn't feel the same.

Talmadge Hall never felt like a place of refuge.

"I live in the Arts District. Have a place that overlooks the river."

"Much more suitable to your life-style, I'm sure," she said stiffly.

Another indication of his success and of how far he'd gone in his quest to move up. For a moment, she wondered what his place looked like. Sleek and modern, she'd bet. With black and gray and chrome.

Sighing softly, she looked at the bottom of the box. They were through the entire year's papers and found no mention of her father or mother.

"Nothing," she said, looking at the dust that covered her shorts, rubbing the grime on her hands.

"Nothing in that year, let's try the earlier one. When exactly did your father leave?"

"I don't know. I was so little. Sometime before Abby was born, but I couldn't tell you exactly when."

They opened the box with papers from twenty-four years ago, and began to delve into it.

"Where do you live now, Caroline?" Brandon asked.

"Actually though I work in Dallas, I live in Fort Worth. A bit less expensive and yet really friendly. I just bought my condo last year."

"Your grandmother didn't mind you moving to Dallas?"

"Actually, she did. I went to visit Jody and then I never came back. You know how crucial appearances were to her. She thought it beneath her granddaughter to work. How she expected each of us to make a living without working is beyond me."

He remembered. He expected Eugenia had planned on rich husbands for her granddaughters. Let the man support them in the style Eugenia so adored. He hadn't fit Eugenia's ideal husband for one of her granddaughters. He was older now and a bit wiser.

"Did Eugenia come from a poor background? Maybe that's why money and class distinction were so important to her."

"Is that why you find it important?" she asked.

He raised his eyes until he stared into hers. "I wanted more than what I started with. Doesn't everyone want to better himself?"

"Maybe, but that's no reason to ignore your family or fight against what's important to them."

"Are we talking about Eugenia or me?"

She shrugged.

"I didn't marry you for money or position."

"Why did you marry me?" she asked, holding her breath for the answer.

"It seemed the thing to do at the time," he replied, holding her gaze with his own. Wondering again, why she'd married him. As an escape from her grandmother's domination?

"What about love?" she asked so softly, he almost missed the words.

"Love's an illusion, a transitory emotion best left to teenagers and dead poets."

For a long moment, she couldn't speak. Her throat ached. She felt the sting of tears behind her lids. The sadness of the years weighed her down. They'd had so much love when they'd started out, how could it ever have gone so wrong?

She licked her lips and looked away. "I should have figured it out then, huh? Especially when you were gone all the time," she said at last.

"Why do you think I worked such long hours? Went without so we could save money to get ahead? I wanted the best for you and instead was only able to give you a third-floor walk-up apartment that contributed to the death of our baby."

"No! I told you last night that had nothing to do with it."

Caroline wanted to say something more about the past, but couldn't find the words. The loss was too great. The longing was something she constantly lived with. She couldn't talk about it.

"Miss Caroline?" Rosalie appeared in the doorway.

"Yes?"

"The appraiser is here."

"I'll be right there."

Scrambling up, she wiped her dusty hands on her shorts, knowing she must look a mess. Well, she wasn't out to impress anyone. She glanced at Brandon and then looked away. Thankful for the interruption, she hurried downstairs.

Brandon watched her go and reluctantly returned to sorting. He needed to focus on his reason for being here and not get sidetracked.

Caroline had become even more beautiful over the years, maturing into a lovely woman. The hint of sadness and mystery in her eyes, her graceful walk, the elegant way she moved her hands when talking only captivated him more.

He didn't wish to be captivated. Once he'd loved her more than life itself. He'd thought she hung the stars. Only to find at the first sign of trouble, she scooted back home and turned her back on him, on that love. On their future.

It proved difficult to concentrate on the task at hand when he had a million questions he wanted to fire off. The primary one being why she hadn't given them a second chance?

Or were the old suspicions true? Had she seen him as an escape from Eugenia only to decide the change wasn't worth the price?

Restless with the pointless questions, he rose and went back to the attic. They'd be finished with that second box in no time. He brought down two more. He thought it extremely unlikely Caroline would find anything incriminating in her grandmother's papers, but he was willing to go along with her for a day or two more. By Sunday, he had to get her signature and head back for New Orleans. His company would only run itself for so long.

Caroline returned a few minutes later, frowning. "He said it may take weeks to get everything appraised. And when I mentioned the furniture in the attic, he upped it by another week."

"Is there any rush?"

She shrugged. "I thought a couple of weeks would see everything wrapped up. Then I could get back to my normal life."

"What did you and your sisters decide about the furnishings? Are you going to sell everything with the house?"

"Not everything. But if a buyer wants what we don't, they can have it. Abby and Michelle told me which pieces they want. The rest I can leave here temporarily. Some pieces are quite valuable. I may be able to sell them to antique dealers. I expect the house will take some time to sell. There's not much market for a huge old antebellum house with all the upkeep it demands. When it sells, any furniture left unsold can be put in storage until I find buyers."

She sat gingerly near the open box, keeping her distance from Brandon.

"There are some very beautiful antiques. And I can offer the buyer a history of each piece. Eugenia told us about them often enough."

A soft chirping sounded.

"What's that?" Caroline looked around, puzzled.

"My phone." Brandon reached into his back pocket and brought out his thin cell phone. He swiped and spoke. "Madison."

Betty Jean's voice responded. "I know you said nothing short of an emergency, but we've got a problem with Bendix again. The timing's getting tight."

"Have Samuels handle it and update me when I get in."

"And that will be?"

"Monday."

"For sure, boss? I've rearranged all your appointments and meetings for Monday. Don't stay longer, it'll play havoc with your calendar."

"That's why I pay you the big bucks, to keep things running smoothly."

She laughed. "Right. I'll remind you of the big bucks scenario come raise time. What are you doing there, boss?"

"Right now, sorting through papers from twenty years ago," he said dryly. "I'll see you Monday."

"Do you want interim updates on this situation?"

"Monday."

He ended the call and slipped the phone into his back pocket.

"I guess we should be glad that's the first time they needed you, huh?" Caroline said dryly.

"I've been in touch since I've been here."

"I'm not surprised. Couldn't let something like a visit interrupt your work, now could we?"

"I run a company, Caroline," he said evenly.

"And it's the most important thing in your life, right?"

"It is now."

She dragged one of the unopened boxes and turned her back to him. He almost smiled at the childish gesture. But her words echoed in the silence.

His work was important. It was the only steadfast certainty. He apparently was not good at relationships— witness his own marriage. But he was outstanding in business endeavors. His rise in the tech industry had been nothing short of meteoric.

Caroline ripped off the old tape and opened the box. This one was from the year her mother died. Quickly she skimmed the pages, sorting, discarding, consciously ignoring the man behind her. She heard the pages ruffle as he worked and fought the temptation to shift her position so she could see him.

Gradually her anger abated. She'd known he was a workaholic from the early days. Why try to fight fate? Brandon was as he was. At one time, she'd supported his dedication, his long hours to build a career. She'd been so proud of him.

So focused was she on denying any interest in Brandon, she almost missed the letter. Only after it was in the discard pile did the words register. She snatched it back. Reading it carefully, she felt the first stirring of enthusiasm.

"Brandon, listen to this," she said excitedly, her momentary pique forgotten.

"It's a letter from—" she turned it over to find a signature "—someone named Edith. Sounds like she was a friend of Eugenia, listen. 'My dear Eugenia. I still am so distressed at Amanda's passing,'" Caroline looked up briefly. "Amanda was my mother."

Brandon nodded. "I remember."

Caroline continued, "'But I suspect you know that. When I think of those three motherless children, I want to weep. And especially because it need not have happened. No matter what you say, I firmly believe your meddling in that marriage was a contributing factor to Amanda's giving up. You were a fool to attempt to play God. She loved Sam and he adored her. The fact he had no money or family background to suit you, was always immaterial. I wonder if your conscience lets you sleep at night.'"

Quickly Caroline skimmed ahead. "The rest of the letter is about some mutual friends. Then she ends it as 'your longtime friend, Edith.'"

Her eyes shining, Caroline looked up. "That's proof, don't you think, that Eugenia did do something!"

"It could indicate that."

"But what? Did she drive him away or did she just meddle in the marriage until he got fed up and left?" she asked, studying the letter again as if it could provide the answer.

"See if there are any more letters from Edith."

"Grandmother probably severed all ties with the woman after that letter. I'm sure she didn't like being taken to task for her behavior. Odd she kept it, isn't it?"

"Unless the other information in the letter was of importance to her. But I'd say it was odd. Yet she probably never expected you to go through these boxes and discover it."

Caroline nodded in agreement. "And I never would have even thought to do so if she hadn't rambled on as she did before she died. I want to see if I can find anything else."

"You may never discover the entire truth," Brandon said.

She looked out the open French doors, gazing over the garden, the stately oaks green and lush, gray Spanish moss dripping from some of the limbs.

"Still, learning the possibility that my father didn't abandon us shook my world," she began slowly. "I thought one of the truths of my life was that he had. I thought everything my grandmother ever told me was the absolute truth. To find out that was such a monumental lie makes me wonder if other things were lies. And if so, what? But the most important part is that maybe my father didn't leave of his own volition, that he didn't deliberately abandon me. I almost can't imagine how that will affect my view of the world. Of relationships."

She darted a quick glance at him.

"And if you find out he didn't want to leave, what then? He's had years to contact you after your mother died. And never did. Gone is gone."

She shrugged. "He could have been killed, moved across the world. Who knows why he didn't get in touch. Maybe there was something Eugenia held over him to prevent his trying. It almost doesn't matter. Just knowing he didn't leave of his own volition but was driven away is enough. For me."

"And will that be enough for Abby and Michelle?"

"What do you mean?"

"Aren't you curious about the man? Don't you want to know where he is, if he's still alive? What he's been doing these last twenty-three years?"

She thought about it seriously for a long moment. "Yes, I would, I guess. But for now that's not as important as knowing he didn't abandon his children. I might be interested in meeting him, talking to him, finding out what he's been doing all this time. But, the important thing to me, is the knowing."

"You need more facts than any papers your grandmother may have saved," Brandon said.

"What else should I be doing?" she asked.

"You could start with talking to contemporaries of your mother or your grandmother. See if anyone has a clue to what happened. For all you know, the situation was common knowledge twenty some years ago." He stretched his arms overhead, then rotated his shoulders, as if stiff from the work.

"My grandmother never spoke of it. She'd always changed the subject if we ever brought it up. Besides, if it were common knowledge, wouldn't someone have told us before now?" she asked, trying to keep her gaze on his face, but she couldn't help be intrigued by the muscles in his arms and chest as he stretched.

He looked solid and big and formidable. Not the striving young man she'd married. He'd come into his own.

For a moment, she felt the sharp prick of regret that they were no longer together. Did he ever wish that he hadn't turned his back on her and let her go?

Did he see other women?

"Now what?" he asked, looking at her sharply.

"Huh?"

"You have the most peculiar look on your face. What are you thinking about?"

"Nothing." She looked down at the letter again.

Brandon stepped across the boxes, dodged the stack of papers now spilling over from the trash and hunkered down beside her. He reached out a finger and tilted her face up to his.

"What?" he asked softly.

"I was wondering if you dated other women," she threw out, amazed at her boldness. It was none of her business.

She was his wife, but they hadn't shared a life since—

"No, I don't date. I'm married, remember? Though, I guess, I'm still surprised that's so."

"What do you mean?"

She tried to ignore the spiraling sensation of awareness his touch started. She wished he'd move his hand, yet craved his touch the way a thirsty man in the desert craved water. Gazing into his eyes, she saw the lines around the edges that hadn't been there five years ago and a poignant realization hit her. They were growing older. Life was moving ahead and the once bright dreams they shared no longer had meaning.

"I'd have thought Eugenia would have prevailed upon you to divorce me years ago."

"She tried."

"And?"

Knocking his hand away, Caroline stood and took a couple of steps toward the balcony. Brandon followed. She wanted to turn and run. He was so close she could imagine the edge of her shorts brushed against his khakis. His breath stirred the air around her face. Swallowing hard, she faced him and gave a halfhearted shrug.

"I didn't want a divorce. It was my independent stand against her. She couldn't force me."

"And now?" His voice hardened a bit.

"Miss Caroline, you and your man coming to lunch? I don't want to throw it out," Rosalie called up the stairs.

"We'll be right there," Caroline yelled back, grateful for the interruption.

She didn't want to talk about divorce, or marriage, or anything. She started to leave but Brandon caught her arm.

"We still need to talk, Caroline."

"Maybe, but I have a million things to do now. And Rosalie is the only one left to help out around here. I don't want to alienate her or I'll have to do everything."

"Being a few minutes late to lunch won't alienate her," he said dryly.

She pulled her arm from his grasp and started walking. "Maybe not, but we can talk later."

Caroline did her best to avoid Brandon that afternoon. She called her office. When Brandon made a comment in passing about die-hard business owners, she flushed. She was as involved in her business as he was in his.

But she could put it aside for family, she thought defensively. If she needed to. Wasn't her presence in

Talmadge Hall proof?

By dinner, Caroline convinced herself she could spend time with Brandon and discuss whatever he wanted rationally, without becoming emotionally upset.

If given the opportunity, would she consider changing her life? Maybe she and Brandon could still build some kind of marriage. Not the way she first expected, but a different kind of relationship. She had her work now. He had his.

If her expectations were lower, if she didn't ever plan to risk another pregnancy, could they build a future together?

Was that what he wanted to discuss? He was staying to help her find the truth about her father. Didn't that show some interest on his part?

By dinner, she was ready for the discussion he kept bringing up, whatever it entailed.

They'd planned to eat on the veranda, in the shade of an old oak tree. She didn't want to eat formally in the dining room every night as her grandmother had. Showering and changing into a pink-and-white sun dress, Caroline was pleased to see some color in her cheeks. She was still too thin, but maybe the dress would camouflage that fact.

Brandon had also changed his clothes, she noted, when she joined him on the veranda. He looked wonderful.

"Did you get a drink?" she asked.

He raised a glass half full of amber liquid. "Iced tea suits me. Can I get you something?"

"No, I'll wait for dinner and have tea as well."

Feeling almost shy, she crossed the veranda to the table Rosalie had prepared. It looked lovely, set with crystal, fine china and silverware. She touched one plate lightly.

"When we were children, Eugenia would never use this china. It's Lennox and she said clumsy little girls had no appreciation for the finer things in life. So we ate off different china."

She lifted the plate and held it up, looking at Brandon with an imp of mischief. "I could smash it now and there'd be nothing she could do about it."

He nodded. "You could, but why bother? She wouldn't know about it, either."

"I guess." Slowly she put the plate down. "We didn't have such a great childhood," she said slowly.

"So I'm coming to find out."

"I used to love to hear you talk about your childhood."

"It wasn't so great, either. We were dirt poor and hard-pressed sometimes to have food on the table."

"But playing in the river, exploring the bayous with your friends, the way your family celebrated the holidays, it sounded like a Brady Bunch family to me. I often wondered what my mother was like. Had she been raised the same way we were or had Eugenia felt she'd done things wrong with her and changed her tactics with us."

Caroline looked at him uncertainly. "She wanted each of us to marry into families with pedigrees back to the Mayflower and with money to burn."

"And instead, you married me."

She nodded, her gaze dropping to the place setting. The silence seemed endless. "And neither of my sisters is married. Both took off from Baton Rouge as soon as they could."

Raising her eyes, she found Brandon's gaze steady on her. She should say something else, but her throat closed and she felt tears welling. Why had they let happiness slip through their fingers? The years since she'd last seen him seemed so lonely, so empty. Nothing had changed, but the sadness that filled her was almost more than she could bear.

"I fixed fried chicken and all the trimmings," Rosalie said, wheeling a tea cart loaded with bowls and platters out onto the veranda. "Now both of you eat up. Don't want this food to go to waste."

"Cold fried chicken is good the next day," Brandon said, holding Caroline's chair. She sat and blinked to dispel the tears. She refused to let them spill over.

"We got plenty other things to eat, don't have to be eating leftovers," Rosalie grumbled as she began to serve dinner.

It was growing dark by the time they finished. Brandon sat back and sighed, a grin lighting his features. "Best eating I've had in a while."

"Do you cook for yourself?" Caroline asked, curious about how he lived. Curious about a lot of things.

"No, I eat out mostly or nuke something."

"I once thought that'd be fun to eat out all the time. But when I first started in Dallas, I did that a lot and it got old fast. I'd rather have a cup of chicken soup in my own place than endless meals out alone. I like my own company."

Brandon nodded. The time couldn't be put off.

"Do you want to walk along the levee?" she asked. "It's not too dark yet and it's pretty along the river in the evening."

"Fine."

He rose and followed her as she wound through the overgrown gardens and up a short pathway to the top of the levee. The Mississippi River drifted lazily by, the water dark and muddy. Most of the light had faded from the sky, stars were showing in the eastern horizon. Before long it'd be pitch-black.

"And when the last of twilight fades, what will keep us from plunging into the water?" Brandon asked as they headed up the bank.

She laughed softly. "There's going to be a full moon soon. It should peek out over that way in only a little while. With the clear sky, it'll give us plenty of light. We don't need city lights for everything," she mocked softly.

"Honey, you're talking with a country boy. Never even saw the city until I was fourteen."

She smiled. "I remember. Stick with me, I'll make sure you don't fall into the river," Caroline said, reaching out to take his hand.

It was a mistake. She knew it as soon as her fingers grasped his, as soon as she felt his fingers slide between hers and his hand grip hers firmly.

The sensations that danced along her nerves had nothing to do with keeping them safe, keeping from plunging into the river. They had to do with love and longing. With memories of things that should have been locked away and only let out in the darkest of midnight in the privacy of her room.

Instead, once again past and present seemed to mingle and Caroline had trouble differentiating between them. She'd loved him so much and had grieved his loss as much as their baby. More—she'd never seen her baby, never held the child. But her arms ached for longing when she slept alone. And hope died slowly when he never attempted to contact her.

But there was anger mixed up in her feelings, anger he hadn't cared enough to come after her. Anger that he'd so easily let her go. If he'd walked out on her—

But of course in a way he had. He'd turned his back and focused on work to the exclusion of everything else.

She hadn't gone after him either. Should she have stayed? Should she have returned after the worst of her grief had eased and forced a confrontation between them? Fought harder for her marriage?

For the first time she looked at her own behavior. For years she'd considered herself wronged. But she was no princess in a locked tower. Had she also wronged Brandon? Marriage was a two-way street. She'd waited for him to come after her, but the conviction suddenly hit her—she should have gone after him.

"Caroline," he began.

"Brandon," she mimicked, turning to look at him.

Was it possible to have a second chance? Was there time to see if they could make a go of it? She'd put away foolish, girlish romantic thoughts. She could enter into an alliance with more realistic expectations now.

"You asked me if I ever thought about you. I thought of you often after you left," he began.

"I thought about you all the time," she confessed.

"I'm afraid to ask how you thought about me."

Should she tell him the truth? Would it matter now after all the years?

"I was devastated at first," she began. "Then I got angry.

"I could tell," he murmured dryly.

"Hush, I'm telling this and don't need interruptions."

He smiled in the darkness. She always liked to talk in the dark. Maybe it had something to do with the way her grandmother raised her. She had to be so proper and controlled where people could see her. But under cover of darkness Caroline could let her true self surface.

Had he made a mistake not coming for her after dark, he wondered whimsically. For a moment he let his imagination roam on what the present would be like if he'd done things differently five years ago.

"I needed you and you weren't there," she said.

"When?"

"All the time," she said. "When I lost the baby. I wasn't even home from the hospital an hour before you left. You were at work when I woke up and when I went to bed at night. At least, I thought you were at work."

His hand tightened on hers. "What does that mean?"

"I don't know. It occurred to me maybe you weren't working, maybe you had—"

"Had what?"

"Other needs? Others who could help you through that time?"

"If you are asking about other women, say so."

"Okay, was there someone else?"

Chapter Five

"Caroline, you're the most exasperating woman I've ever known. I can't believe you'd ever think such a thing!"

"It's not hard. Why else would you be gone all the time?"

Brandon dragged his fingers through his hair and turned to stare at the slow-moving river.

"I blamed myself for the loss of our baby. If we'd had more money we wouldn't have lived there. Throwing myself into work was my way of dealing with the situation. Next time, I vowed, there'd be no third-floor apartment. You'd have the best care money could buy!"

"I told you living there had no impact. The doctor was clear there was nothing we could have done. That precious baby was just not meant to be born. I railed against fate for months, inconsolable. But that didn't change anything." She stopped for a moment, then took a deep breath. "I loved our apartment. It was my first real home."

"And that wasn't," he said nodding back toward the mansion.

"No. It was a place I lived with my grandmother. It was her home, her avocation almost, but to me it was just a place to stay while I was growing up. Our apartment was the first place I truly felt at home."

He ducked his head trying to see into her eyes. "I never knew that."

She shrugged. "You should have. I did all I could to make it nice for us."

"It was a home. And cold as ice once you left. I couldn't stay when I finally realized you weren't coming back. Everything there reminded me of you."

Caroline knew she owed Brandon the truth she'd just realized.

"I shouldn't have waited for you to come after me. It was my marriage, too. I realize now, that I should have fought for it. But at the time, I thought that if you came after me it would prove that you cared. I was young. Still had fairy tale ideas about marriage, I guess."

He sighed and rubbed his eyes with his thumb and forefinger. "I don't think I could offer you enough assurances. I tried, but obviously failed."

Slowly, she reached up and touched his cheek lightly with her fingertips.

"I was only twenty-one. A kid really. And kids that young shouldn't have to face life-and-death problems like we did. I was too young to know that time gradually heals everything—even the loss of a baby. Though not completely. I wake sometimes in the night and think I hear an infant crying. My arms longed to hold that baby, my heart still aches with the loss. She'd have been almost five, starting kindergarten in the fall."

"So you think it was a girl?"

"I don't know. Sometimes I imagine a little boy."

"Don't think about it, honey. It'll tear you apart if you keep dwelling on it."

"I know that. I discovered that in the first months afterward. But sometimes I just can't help myself."

He drew her into his embrace, holding her close to his heart, rubbing her back slowly. It was meant to comfort, Caroline knew. But the feel of Brandon's arms around her didn't soothe, but excited.

She drew in a breath, surrounded by his scent, enticing and male.

She wanted more than comfort. She wanted affirmation that he'd thought about her over the years. That he'd wanted her with the same longing and remembered fever with which she ached for him.

She tilted up her head, wishing that it wasn't so dark, wishing she could see his expression, look into his eyes and see what he was feeling.

"I'm glad you came after all," she whispered.

When he lowered his face to kiss her, she responded eagerly.

So familiar, so different.

She kissed him with all the longing of five long empty years. Giving no thought to the future, Caroline plunged herself into the present. She'd been too long without the feel of a man's arms around her, without the exquisite zinging in her blood, without the sensations that brought her to life as nothing else ever had. She'd missed Brandon, and his touch, his special excitement.

The kiss went on so long Caroline lost track of time and place. Brandon anchored her to earth or carried her to the stars, she wasn't sure which. Eons passed or time stood still. They were alone in the world or in a world of their own making, where everything was possible, and nothing had the power to hurt.

When Brandon slowly lifted his head, searching her face, touching her lips lightly, she was dropped back into reality.

"Stay with me tonight," he said, his hands molding her to him.

Shocked at the suggestion, she hesitated. There was so much between them. Nothing had changed. Would taking such a step he proposed solve anything? Or make it worse?

Yet when he held her, she could scarcely think. Only feel. Feel the pleasure her husband always gave her. Feel the fire in her blood that ignited only when he touched her. Feel connected, safe, free.

How could anything be worse than the separation they'd endured? Maybe it was time to let go of the past and try again. Excitement flared. Swallowing hard, feeling daring and alive for the first time in years, she slowly nodded.

They walked back to the house, awareness between them strong, the knowledge of what they were about to do acting as an aphrodisiac. Despite the darkness, Caroline found the path with no difficulty, feeling as if she were floating above the sandy surface.

Not two minutes earlier, she'd wished for more light, but the brightness in the house seemed harsh after the soft moonlight on the levee. For a moment, she panicked. Did she know what she was doing? She hadn't seen Brandon in five years. They'd separated under the worst of circumstances.

But when he brushed his lips against hers again, she knew the fever in her blood couldn't be quenched. She had so little, a night in his arms would hurt no one. Even if he didn't stay, even if business proved a stronger pull, she'd have one more memory. A happier one, to replace some of the sad ones.

He led her into his room and shut the door. With a muffled groan, he snatched her close and hugged her so tightly she could scarcely breathe. This was where she belonged. Did Brandon know they belonged together? He couldn't be so loving if he didn't feel it, too.

When he picked her up and gently laid her on the bed, Caroline forgot to think. Ignoring her doubts, she knew only that she wanted him more than anything. Craved his touch, longed for the passion she knew she'd find in his arms. The past was gone. Maybe they could forge a new future together.

As he lay down on the bed beside her, she smiled shyly and reached out to draw him closer. For the first time in years, Caroline felt she'd come home.

The chirping of Brandon's phone woke her. It was just after dawn and the sky was a soft blue. Cool air stirred through the open French doors. Caroline rolled her head and looked at him, her heart kicking into overdrive. He lay beside her and looked so dear she could scarcely breathe. She wanted to find the phone and smash it to smithereens. He'd wake up any second and be drawn into the call from his business.

He opened his eyes and gazed into hers.

The chirping sounded louder, more insistent.

"Good morning," he said, brushing a kiss across her lips.

Before she could respond, Brandon rolled over and sat up, reaching for the phone. The move dislodged the sheet and Caroline scrambled to pull it over her. This wasn't how she'd envisioned waking up.

They'd made love often when they lived together, yet the bold light of day made her feel as shy as their first time so long ago.

"Madison," he said. "And this had better be good or you're fired."

Betty Jean had been with him for almost five years. She knew when to call and when not to, but frustration built. One glance at Caroline and he knew she had the same thoughts she always did about his work. And this time he wasn't sure he could blame her.

"Boss, it's not good. Bendix is threatening to go to the newspapers and claim we ripped him off with the software and it's all scam. Joe can't handle all the details and Martin doesn't have your clout."

"Blast it all!"

He pushed back the covers and stood, walking to the window. It was just after dawn, far earlier than he'd wanted to wake up.

"Sorry to cut your weekend short."

"I'll be there as soon as I can make it."

He disconnected and turned to look at Caroline. The frown on her face assured him she'd heard his comment and was clearly unhappy.

"I have to go," he said.

"Go," she said, looking away.

Her hands balled into fist on the sheet. Nothing changed. Why had she thought a night together would change everything.

"I didn't plan this. There's a major problem with one of our largest clients. I've got to get to the office to assess the situation, real and potential, and then see what we can do to minimize any fall out."

"So go," she said. "There's no one here stopping you."

"Look at me."

He strode over to the bed and leaned across it, putting his face almost against hers. Slowly she turned and looked at him, her eyes wide and impassive.

"Don't pout," he said, wanting to kiss those slightly swollen lips, change her frown to that slumberous look she got when they made love. But there wasn't enough time.

"I'll be back as soon as I can," he said, leaning another few inches to brush her lips with his.

"Don't bother," she said. "I'll finish the search on my own. And I certainly can manage my own life without your help. I have for five years."

Brandon straightened and ran a hand through his hair in frustration. Turning, he reached in the drawers for a change of clothes. He still had a couple of new shirts and another pair of khakis. He headed for the bathroom.

Caroline could almost see his mind already spinning making preliminary plans for damage control.

Caroline waited until he closed the bathroom door before venturing from the bed. She found her sundress, in a puddle on the floor where she'd discarded it last night. Drawing it on, she looked at the tousled bed.

Last night had been wonderful.

If his office hadn't called, would they have made love again?

Nothing had been said about the future, but before falling asleep, Caroline envisioned today totally differently.

Instead of reading musty old papers, she'd have suggested a long picnic in the lazy afternoon sunshine. Maybe dinner and dancing in downtown Baton Rouge, she thought wistfully.

"Daydreams aren't worth the paper they're written on," she quoted wryly.

Turning resolutely, she knew she couldn't daydream away her life. He was leaving. That was that.

She knocked against the chair holding his suit jacket. As it slid to the floor, she smiled sadly. When they'd lived together, he'd always slung his jacket on the back of any available chair, leaving it to her to hang it in the closet.

Sighing wryly, she admitted old habits were hard to break. She reached down to pick it up. A batch of folded papers fell from his inside pocket. Her name on the partially folded sheet caught her eye. Slowly, she picked up the pages and opened the packet. Skimming the front page, she sank to the edge of the bed in shock.

Divorce papers! That had been the reason he'd shown up. She shouldn't be surprised.

Embarrassed heat flooded her as she realized what a mistake last night had been.

She'd been entertaining thoughts that they might try to get back together, might try to make their marriage work.

Instead Brandon had come to ask her for a divorce!

An incredible hurt began to sweep through her. He'd never hinted at the real reason for his visit. Last night had seemed so special and, gullible as a teenager, she'd gone along with his every suggestion.

Gone along? She'd practically thrown herself at him. No wonder he'd said nothing.

"I'll call you—"

Brandon stopped in the doorway, his eyes on her face. When he dropped his gaze to the papers in her lap, his expression closed.

"You'll call me about the divorce? Was that what you were going to say?" she asked. Slowly her hand rose to massage her heart. She knew it was breaking—again.

Was that possible?

"Caroline, honey, I—"

She rose, enraged. "Don't honey me, you lying rat! You never did say why you showed up this week, did you? What was last night about? You came here for a divorce. Was last night just a final fling?"

She threw the papers at him. Brandon didn't move and the sheets drifted to the floor. Caroline stepped over them as she stormed for the door.

"Don't leave!" he ordered.

She turned to glare at him. "I don't have to leave. If I wait long enough you'll do that for us, right? Go to your precious business. And don't ever come back."

"Caroline."

"Shut up!"

Horrified at what she'd discovered, horrified that she'd misjudged the situation so much, Caroline spun around and ran down the hall to her own room, slamming the door shut behind her as the tears spilled over.

She hadn't cried in front of him. A small victory, but all she seemed to have right now.

Last night had been glorious.

But was she the only one to think so?

He'd come for a divorce. Feeling betrayed, she crossed the room to her own bathroom, locking the door behind her. She had no reason to think he'd come after her, his track record proved that. But just in case. She reached for a towel and sank on the edge of the tub. Her heart was breaking. Sobbing, she tried for control. It was too much. Too much.

"Caroline." He rapped on the door, tried the knob. "Caroline, let me in."

She held her breath, trying to stop the tears. It wasn't like Brandon to come after her. Didn't he have to be at work? Wouldn't his precious business fold without his constant attention?

He knocked harder on the door. "Caroline, I can't leave you like this."

She took a shaky breath, fighting for control. "Go, Brandon. Go away."

"Caroline, this is a major crisis. I have to be there."

"Go away and don't ever come back."

Endless minutes passed. Tears welled again, spilled over her cheeks. She blotted them with the damp towel. She couldn't go through this again. Why hadn't he told her that first afternoon? Why let her begin to dream about—?

"I have to go, but I'm coming back. You can count on that."

The day dragged by. Caroline ignored the stack of papers awaiting her. Ignored the other tasks that had to be done to prepare the house for sale. By the end of the day, she'd accomplished nothing.

Sinking listlessly on one of the wicker rockers on the veranda, she waited for Rosalie to call her to supper. The late-afternoon air was still and hot. Idly staring at the overgrown yard, Caroline ignored it all. Her emotions were all topsy-turvy—anger, hurt, regret.

How could she have allowed herself to be tempted by Brandon?

How could she help it? He tempted her beyond her ability to resist, obviously.

Shaking her head to dislodge those kind of thoughts, she vowed to forget him. He'd returned to his first love, one with whom she couldn't compete. The sooner she got things squared away and returned to her own life, the better she'd be.

And that included forgetting how irresponsibly she'd behaved last night.

The house phone rang. Despite her newfound intentions, her heart leaped. Was it Brandon?

She went swiftly to the hall phone. "Hello."

"Hi, sis, how are you doing?" Abby asked.

Trying to ignore the flare of disappointment, Caroline forced some enthusiasm into her voice.

"I'm doing all right. I didn't expect you to use this phone."

"Well, I called your cell a couple of times today and it always went to voice mail."

Caroline thought a moment. "I think I let the battery run down." She wasn't even sure where her phone was.

"So are you making any headway?" Abby asked.

"The appraiser came yesterday. He says it'll take a while, and he wants to do a room by room assessment. He's bringing a whole battery of appraisers, since each of them has a different area of expertise. I thought they could do it in a few days but they say it may take weeks."

"Is Brandon still there?"

Caroline went still. "No," she said shortly.

"Oh. I thought he was staying through the weekend, at least."

"There was an emergency at work. And work always comes first with Brandon."

"So, uh, did you and he talk some."

"Of course," Caroline said dryly, knowing where her sister was heading. "He was a guest in the house. Did you think I'd ignore him?"

"I mean about, you know, your marriage. About getting back together."

"Nothing's changed."

Except for her entire world being turned upside down in the space of one night.

But Caroline didn't plan to tell anyone that. Especially not her romantic sister. She'd be crushed to learn Brandon had arrived solely to start divorce proceedings.

"I have a couple of days off in the middle of next week. I can come up and help you sort things or whatever," Abby said.

Caroline was tempted, but suspected she should refuse. She didn't want to tell her sisters about their grandmother's revelation until she knew for certain whether it were true or not. Until then, it'd be better for her to do the sorting.

"Not much to do until the appraisals are finished," she said. "Once that's done, I'll have the items you tagged ready to be shipped to you when the house sells."

"I have a friend who has a truck so I'll bring them back myself. I didn't want that much. Sell the rest of that stuff and make us a mint! Michelle and I'll do our share spending all that lovely loot. No sense cluttering up my small apartment with grandmother's antiques. I don't like the memories most of them bring."

Abby chatted for a few more minutes.

Caroline was smiling by the end. Her sister's call had raised her spirits.

Glancing up the stairs, she was tempted to go to Brandon's room. She wondered for the hundredth time what Brandon did with the papers she'd thrown at him that morning. She ought to go up to see if they still lay on the floor or if he'd taken them back with him.

The phone rang again making her jump.

"Hello?"

"Caroline?" It was Brandon.

Immediately she tightened up, the urge to slam down the receiver was strong. How perverse—she wanted him to call, but now she was afraid of what he'd say.

"What?"

"I wanted to see if you're all right."

"I'm fine. Goodbye."

"Wait! I thought you'd like to know about the situation here. There turns out to be a major glitch in the software patch sent to fix another problem. It wasn't beta tested because we rushed the patch through. The result now is I have a major customer mad as he can get. The thing is, I have appointments this week that I really can't postpone."

"So?"

"So, I can't be with you for the next few days." The edge to his voice warned her he was becoming impatient.

"I don't expect you to be with me at all. You have no obligation here."

She hated she'd been badly burned once by this man. She'd be living in a fool's paradise to ever allow herself the slightest glimmer of hope that things could go back the way they'd once been.

"I'll be back as soon as I can make it."

The sincerity almost convinced her there might be a chance.

Almost.

"There's no reason to come back, Brandon. Goodbye."

Slowly, despite his protest, she ended the call.

Giving into curiosity, Caroline climbed the stairs and went to the guest room Brandon had used. The door was open, the bed made. Obviously Rosalie had not let things slide. The room looked immaculate. There were no papers anywhere.

So, she wondered as she headed back downstairs, had he taken them to use for an excuse to see her again? Or had Rosalie picked them up and put them someplace.

Why had he come? He could have mailed them.

The following weekend Michelle arrived to help with the task of packing up Eugenia's personal things.

Caroline had done as much as she could sorting the boxes from the attic. She was glad for her sister's company and was strongly tempted to tell her about her suspicions, about the wild tale Eugenia had told. But she refrained as she had with Abby. No sense all of them worrying about what Eugenia might or might not have done.

They packed up their grandmother's clothes and donated everything still serviceable to a women's shelter. Going through her books they'd put aside the first editions to sell. The rest, and Caroline was surprised at how many books there were on the history of Mississippi and Louisiana, they donated to the library.

Michelle refrained from bringing up Brandon's name until supper on Sunday.

"Heard from Brandon?" she asked, sitting opposite Caroline at the dining-room table.

Caroline shook her head and deliberately took a bite of the delicious shrimp salad Rosalie had prepared.

"Abby said he'd been called back unexpectedly because of some crisis?" Michelle persisted.

Caroline nodded, taking a sip of iced tea. She reached for a hot roll and began to butter it.

"Caroline," Michelle said exasperated, "what's the scoop?"

"No scoop. He came, helped out until work called, then left. End of story."

Michelle thought a moment, watching her sister carefully. Shaking her head slowly she said, "There's more. Spill it."

Caroline considered it. She truly thought she could tell her without breaking down, without revealing how for a few brief hours she'd thought about changing her life.

But she didn't want her sisters to feel sorry for her. Not a second time.

"That's it. Did I tell you that Grandmother's attorney called me on Friday? I asked him to get all the papers together that I need to sign. There's something else he wants to discuss with me, something important apparently. He didn't want to discuss it on the phone. I'm to see him on Wednesday."

"If you don't mind handling it, Abby and I will be guided by whatever you decide."

"I don't mind. I can't think of what he wants to talk about. I wish the appraisers would finish so we can list the house."

"Do you think it'll sell fast?" Michelle asked.

"Nope. It'll take a special person, one with money and who wouldn't mind all the upkeep required," Caroline said.

Michelle glanced around the elegant dining room and wrinkled her nose. "One of us should have felt some attachment to this place."

"Do you ever wonder what our lives would have been like if our father hadn't left and mama hadn't died when Abby was born?" Caroline asked slowly.

"When he deserted us, you mean? When I was little I used to pretend he came back and took us away from Eugenia. And let me stay up late to watch TV."

Caroline smiled. Maybe she wasn't the only one affected by their father's absence.

"I always felt it was my fault he left," she said.

Michelle laughed. "That's dumb, sis. You were about four, right? I was still a baby. How could we have done anything to make a grown man leave?"

"I know that as an adult, but as a kid that's what I thought. And I worried about my bad blood."

"What bad blood?" Michelle asked, puzzled.

"Once I had biology and understood how babies came to be made, and listening to Eugenia harp on lineage and bad blood and the mistake our mother made marrying our father, I worried that I took after him and had bad blood."

"Right, like we could believe anything grandmother said. She was fanatical on the mistake Mom made marrying the man. But she was the only one who thought that marriage was a mistake and only because she wanted her daughter to marry some rich man she'd picked out for her. And it's evident that our father wasn't rich enough."

"As a teenager, I wondered if Mama died of a broken heart."

The knocker on the front door rapped.

Michelle looked up. "Expecting company?"

Caroline shook her head.

Rosalie used the main hall to get to the door. Caroline looked at Michelle and strained to hear who it was.

Two seconds later Brandon walked into the dining room.

Rosalie came right behind him, her face beaming.

"Now you just sit down and I'll bring you a plate right away. I know you must be starving with that long drive from New Orleans. We've got plenty of food. And I know you'll want iced tea. Sit right here."

She pulled out the chair next to Caroline. "I'll be right back."

With a bright grin, she scurried into the kitchen.

Brandon greeted Michelle, then Caroline, sitting in the chair Rosalie had drawn out.

"What are you doing here?" Caroline asked, stunned to see him.

Stunned at the delight that swept through her.

She flicked a glance at Michelle who stared at her in surprise. Taking a deep breath, she pinned a polite smile on her face. "I didn't expect you."

Brandon nodded, amusement evident in his gaze. "I told you I'd be back as soon as I could rearrange it. Finished up everything pressing this morning, which frees me up for the next couple of days. Nice to see you again, Michelle. Will you be joining us in searching?"

"Searching?"

"No, Michelle's leaving after supper," Caroline said, narrowing her eyes in an attempt to head Brandon away from that dangerous topic. "We've done lots this weekend— sorted Eugenia's clothes. We gave the usable items to a shelter and threw away the rest. Although, we did keep two old dresses to use as rags. We threw out the ones that no one could wear. Dumped her cosmetics and personal items."

"And the books, don't forget the books, Caroline," Michelle said, laughing softly.

When her sister looked at her, she raised her eyebrows in feigned innocence. "I don't know why Brandon needs a play-by-play account of our weekend, but if you're going to give it to him, be precise."

"Oh."

Caroline felt like an idiot. Grateful for Rosalie's interruption when she arrived with a heaping plate for Brandon, she took a sip of iced tea hoping to gain some control over her wayward emotions.

Seeing Brandon was not conducive to serenity.

As she studied him, her heart rate sped up. Her mind filled with images of the two of them the last night he'd been there.

Today, his dark hair looked windblown. His suit fit perfectly, giving him a distinguished appearance that had her flustered. She had trouble thinking straight. Why couldn't the man have stayed in New Orleans?

She couldn't very well kick him out while Michelle was

sitting there. The questions would be endless. But as soon as her sister left, she'd have it out with Brandon Madison. If he'd brought his blasted divorce papers, she'd sign them and send him on his way tonight!

Michelle seemed reluctant to leave. When they'd finished dinner, she suggested they sit on the veranda for a while. She and Brandon easily discussed various topics. Caroline threw in a comment from time to time to keep her sister from suspecting anything was wrong, but as the evening progressed she wanted to scream her frustration.

The later it got, the harder it'd be to get rid of Brandon.

Even now, it was almost too late for anyone to reach New Orleans at a reasonable hour.

"Oh, look at the time, I must go," Michelle said, as if reading her sister's mind. "This has been great, Brandon. I'm so glad we got to visit for a while."

Brandon stood as Michelle did. "Can I help you with your bags?"

"Thanks, but I only had a small tote and put it in the car before supper. I'd say don't be a stranger, but I don't think I need to say that now, right?" she asked, glancing between the two of them.

Fortunately, Caroline thought, Brandon kept silent. She gave a small smile and remained quiet herself. Time enough to explain things to her sisters later, after she clarified everything with Brandon.

"Goodbye, Caroline, let me know what happens with the attorney." Michelle gave her a hug and then surprised Caroline by giving Brandon a brief hug. "See you."

Caroline remained silent as her sister started her car and drove down the driveway.

Finally, she stood and faced the man who was driving her crazy. "You have a nerve coming back."

"I'm happy to see you again, too, sweetheart," he said, then pulled her close and kissed her.

Caroline resisted—for about two seconds.

But the seductive pull of his touch proved stronger than her resolve. When his lips moved persuasively, she succumbed and responded. No matter what else happened between the two of them, this never changed. Delighted in the feel of the man, in the strong beat of his heart beneath her palm, the feel of his hard muscles beneath her fingertips. Shocked with her easy capitulation, she sought the strength to push against that hard chest.

When he released her, she stared up at him, her eyes wide and furious. She wanted to be angry with him, but some of that anger was directed toward herself.

"Don't do that!"

"I like doing that. And by your response, you like it, too."

"That has nothing to do with anything," she snapped, turning to put some distance between them.

"I beg to differ. I think it shows there is still something between us."

"After the other night, I think that would be obvious. But it's only sex."

She didn't want to discuss the other night, but better she bring it up first. Maybe she could control the trend of the conversation. "That was never a problem area in our marriage. Speaking of which, did you bring the divorce papers back with you?"

"Not this trip. I want to talk with you first."

"You sound like a broken record. That's all you say. Where were you five years ago when I wanted to talk? There's nothing to say now."

"I think there is. Your response has me thinking things might not be over. That we might salvage something."

"Like what? You have your work and now I have a life in Dallas."

"So maybe your own business gives you a better understanding of the demands that can arise. I won't apologize for working hard. I wanted more for you and that was the only way I knew how to get it."

She spun around at that. "Oh, Brandon, that was never what I wanted. I grew up with money. It bought things, but things are meaningless when a person craves something else. I wanted a family. I wanted to be important to you, have you find me important."

"I did."

Remembering her thoughts of a different kind of marriage, she wondered if Brandon might be thinking along similar lines. A marriage that'd allow them to be together, but without the high and unrealistic expectations they'd once had.

"Why, after all this time, do you want a divorce?" she asked.

He rubbed the back of his neck and loosened his tie. Staring out over the shaggy green lawn he spoke softly. "I was advised to get one by my attorney."

She blinked in surprise. "Your attorney? Why?"

He drew a breath. The reason couldn't be any worse than the actual demand, she tried to tell herself as her apprehension grew the longer he took to answer.

"My company's ready to expand. We'll be moving into an entire new strata with the potential to reap a tremendous profit. Greg suggested I take steps to make sure I keep what I earn."

She stared at him for a moment, until the meaning sank in.

"So rather than take the chance your wife would come storming in to demand half of all that lovely profit, your attorney advised you to get rid of her, now, while you're still relatively poor?"

Brandon looked at her, his expression unreadable. He nodded, once, wondering why he'd given into Greg's suggestion. In all the years they'd been separated, Caroline had never once asked for a dime. She'd had her grandmother's wealth to fall back on. She hadn't needed anything he could give her. That thought rankled.

Even now, once the estate was settled, Caroline would inherit one third. The furnishings in the dining room alone would bring a tidy sum. He couldn't imagine her ever wanting anything from him.

Yet that didn't mean it wasn't prudent to protect his assets.

"You should've brought the papers—I'd sign them in a heartbeat," she said, walking past him and into the house.

Chapter Six

Brandon let out his breath in a long sigh. After spending that night with Caroline, all the old feelings began to tumble around inside. Dare they consider working out some arrangement where they'd stay married, even be together from time to time?

He shook his head. He'd missed her this last week more than he'd expected. Especially at night when he lay alone in that king-size bed, he'd bought a few years ago. Instead of instantly falling asleep each night, he'd lain awake and thought about Caroline. How soft her skin had felt, her hair like silk. Remembering not just their most recent night together, but others as well.

Closing his eyes, standing on the veranda surrounded with the scent of sweet jasmine, and despite the cool breeze from the river, he swore he could still smell Caroline's fragrance.

Spinning around, he went to his car and withdrew the large suitcase. He was staying until they'd hashed everything out and came to a resolution. He hoped it'd be one he'd want to live with.

Caroline heard Brandon's steps on the stairs, the sound

of a door closing. He was staying. She was puzzled as to why he planned to stay despite her obvious lack of welcome.

He was the most determined man—focused on whatever goal he set for himself. Look how he'd risen from his poor beginnings to the successful businessman he was today. So successful, his attorney feared for his wife's greedy hand in his affairs.

Dressing quickly for bed, Caroline slipped between the sheets and snapped off her light. Lying alone in the dark, she felt the siren pull of Brandon's presence only a few doors down the hall. Closing her eyes for sleep didn't help. Behind her lids, she saw that night a week ago. She could almost feel Brandon's fingertips against her skin, his lips on hers. She kicked off the sheet, suddenly hot. The gentle air stirring from the open French doors caressed her skin, as his kisses had.

Rolling on her side, she curled up into a tight ball, wishing her mind would go blank.

"Caroline?"

The soft voice came from the upper balcony that wrapped the house.

"Go away, I'm asleep," she muttered, trying to ignore the pull of attraction.

"Come out and talk to me. There're advantages to this weather. The night's balmy and quiet and I'm too keyed up after that drive to sleep right away."

"That's not my problem," she said, but sat up. Where had she put her robe?

"Come talk to me in the dark," he coaxed.

"In the dark?"

She found the light cotton robe and slipped into it. Flicking her hair out of the neckline, she buttoned it. The floor felt cool beneath her feet as she stepped out onto the wooden balcony. Brandon leaned against the railing, dimly lighted by the stars and the moon that had risen a short time before.

"Why bother to talk. I tell you to go and you ignore me," she said.

"Or, I tell you I'm staying and all you do is argue."

She shrugged and crossed to the railing, careful to keep a wide distance between them. "We didn't used to argue."

"You used to chastise me for being away for long stretches."

"I told you I wanted a husband, not a large paycheck."

"I remember taking long walks together along the river," he said softly, moving closer.

Caroline nodded, watching him warily. She remembered the walks, too. Hands entwined, shoulders brushing as they strolled along the river side and spoke of dreams and plans. Such happy times.

The familiar ache began.

"If I tallied all the things I liked about being married to you, it would probably take me until Thursday," he said whimsically.

Caroline looked at him in astonishment. That didn't sound like a ruthless businessman.

"What an incredibly nice thing to say!"

"It's true. And I could tally what I didn't like in two

sentences. I regret not having enough money to give you a life similar to the one in which you'd been raised. And I regret each minute I spent away from you."

Staring in disbelief, Caroline could scarcely trust her ears. Was she hearing him correctly? The honeyed words soothed the ache.

"Then why didn't you come after me when I left? Or called or something?" she asked. If he had truly cared, how could he have let her go?

"I was hurting, too. Did you think I didn't love that baby we'd made? Did you think it meant nothing to me to lose it? To know I wouldn't be a father after all. That I wouldn't be helping my child to grow and learn. To see the wonder in his or her eyes as all the magic of living unfolded? That my dad probably wouldn't see a grandchild?"

She shook her head.

"I wanted to do something, but when I tried to talk to you, you'd just shake your head and change the subject. You shut me out, Caroline."

"I didn't shut you out," she protested, even when the doubts arose.

"It sure seemed like it."

Caroline felt dazed. Was his obsession with work truly the result of a wife who'd turned from him?

She'd been so devastated, so inconsolable. Losing her baby had been the hardest, most tragic event of her life. She'd felt so alone. How could she not have known her husband was grieving as well; that he needed more from her than she offered?

"I'm sorry, Brandon."

He nodded. "Grief is handled differently with different people."

"We should've known that. Maybe—" She stopped. What could she say?

"I spent a lot of my free time with my folks after you left. And with my mother after my dad died. She's a wise woman. She helped me work through the grief of losing you and the baby. Too bad the young aren't taught that before we need it. It'd make life a lot easier."

Caroline wrapped one arm around the tall pillar and gazed toward the river.

"You were lucky to have your mother. Eugenia kept telling me to get over it and move on. My sisters were no help, except to be there for support. It was so hard. Even today—"

"I know, the echoes of a crying baby when you awake in the dark."

When his arm encircled her shoulders, Caroline let go the pillar and rested against his chest. It felt so good to be held. To be able to tell him some of what she felt.

"Even today the desolation creeps into me." She realized something else. "I understand now how work can provide a kind of numbing solace." Hadn't she used her own business to try to forget Brandon when she moved to Dallas?

"With all your mother talked to you about, did she ever suggest you see me again?" Caroline asked, curious despite herself.

He shifted on the railing, turning to lean against it,

drawing her into the circle of his arms.

"Not after that last rejection. She said maybe I was beating a dead horse and it was time to let you go."

"What last rejection?" she asked. "I never rejected you."

"What would you call refusing to take my calls, not answering my letters and having a maid tell me you weren't home when I'd seen you enter the house only moments before?" he asked evenly. "I call that blatant rejection."

Caroline felt confused. She leaned back in his arms searching his face. "I don't know what you're talking about."

Instantly Brandon realized.

"Oh, blast it! Eugenia!" he said angrily.

"What?"

"I called that first evening when I got home and you were gone. Eugenia answered the phone and told me you didn't want to talk to me. I called every day for two weeks. I told you I had commitments. I couldn't leave, but I wasn't ignoring you, I called every night! Either Eugenia or some maid named Naomi answered the phone. The message was always the same—you didn't wish to speak to me. I left endless messages asking you to call me."

Caroline shook her head, horrified by what she was hearing. "No, that's not possible. No one gave me any messages."

She clutched his arms. This couldn't be true.

Grimly he nodded. "I called you daily for over a month. I actually came to the house three times and sent you at least five letters—and you know how much I hate to write letters."

Swallowing hard, she knew her world had been shaken again. And by her grandmother's machinations.

"So you did come after me. I never knew," she said, trying to take it all in.

"I never suspected your grandmother to lie. I believed what she said. I wanted to see you, to talk to you, hold you. I was dying inside. We'd lost our baby and then I was losing my wife. Each time that Naomi answered the door she said you weren't at home and she didn't know when to expect you."

"You should have challenged her story."

"I did the time I saw you enter just ahead of me. I pushed my way inside. Eugenia showed up. Your grandmother said you blamed me for everything. Your infatuation had worn off and you wanted out of the relationship. When I heard nothing from you as the days went by, I began to believe her."

Caroline sagged against him, resting her head against his chest.

Futile anger surged.

How had she dared? Eugenia knew how much she missed Brandon. She'd argued with her about it for weeks. And all the time Brandon had been trying to reach her. Her heart broke.

Tears welled. How could her own grandmother have conspired to keep her from her husband?

Was history repeating itself? Had her mother longed for her father when he went away due to Eugenia?

"I started to return to New Orleans a few weeks after

coming here but she convinced me it'd be a mistake. If you cared anything about me, she insisted, you'd have contacted me. In a strange way, it made sense, so I went along with it. For a long time I didn't think too clearly. I was so grief stricken."

Brandon placed a finger beneath her chin and raised her head, resting his forehead on hers.

"We were both deceived."

"And our lives changed because of her. Just like my parents'. How could she have done that?"

Guilt began to build. She should have contacted Brandon, fought harder for her marriage.

After five years was it too late?

"I can't believe it. How dare she play God with people's lives!" Caroline said.

She was furious with her grandmother. Yet, had she not rambled so much when she was so sick, would Caroline believe what Brandon said?

She knew with certainty that Brandon wasn't lying to her now.

"So where do we go from here?" she asked, feeling bereft of everything, uncertain, unsure, numb.

Nothing in her life was proving to be the way she thought it'd been. Would she discover that she could love again? Or would the fear of loss, fear of his turning away, of putting work first always still stand between them?

"Where do you want to go from here?" Brandon asked, releasing her and turning to rest his palms against the railing.

"I'm not sure. I need some time to think about this. I

feel as if my life has been turned upside down."

"But there's more, right?" he asked.

Caroline hated to respond. She wished she could slip back into her bed and pull the covers over her head. Try to discover how she really felt about all this. But she owed Brandon honesty, at least. Especially after her grandmother's lies.

"You came here a couple of weeks ago to seek a divorce. I'm willing to sign the papers to grant you that divorce," she said slowly. "I certainly wouldn't contest it. Learning this about my grandmother changes everything. I feel you got the raw end of the deal. I can't understand her."

She'd startled him, she could tell.

"It's all a jumble, but if you want to proceed, I won't fight it. The circumstances are far different from what I always thought. I'm at fault. I didn't know you tried to reach me. But I know I didn't reach out to you. You were right, I ran. A few weeks after I left New Orleans, I went to visit Jody. I didn't leave Dallas for a few years."

"And now?"

She thought about it for a minute.

"We had a wonderful seven months as a married couple. I loved being married to you, loved every moment until I lost the baby. But that time's gone. Things have happened over the last five years to change us. We aren't the same people we were then. And my grandmother did a horrible thing."

"You're not responsible for her actions. Or did your love die with the baby?"

"No. Not then."

"But later?"

"I don't know," she said, distressed anew. "I thought I was over you. I've made a comfortable life in Dallas.

Had her love died because she thought him uncaring? Or had it only lay dormant—awaiting his presence to spring to life again.

Why couldn't she think straight?

He was silent for a long time.

"Very well then. But if we're getting that divorce, I think we should make some memories to last us down the long lonely years."

He swept her into his arms and kissed her. When he raised his head, she was breathless.

"Sleep with me tonight," he urged.

She was tempted. Standing in the circle of his arms, she felt she could forget everything—the past, the present and the future. But she couldn't spend the rest of her life in his embrace.

She had to get her own life straight before she could think of any future.

"Brandon," Caroline began. She mustn't do this, not again. She could not make love with him tonight and say farewell in the morning.

"Hush," he said as his mouth came down on hers and swept away the doubts.

"I can't."

Pulling free, she fled to her bedroom and shut the French doors with a bang. Despite her best intentions, it was a long time before she fell asleep.

Caroline awoke early. For a moment she was disoriented, until memories returned.

The more she learned about her grandmother, the more angry she grew. The woman had likely ruined five lives, those of her mother, her sisters, her husband and herself. Her actions had been egregious. Was there anyway to mitigate them?

Brandon sat at the top of the stairs the next morning, waiting when Caroline left her room.

"Sleep well?" he asked.

"Fine."

She refused to confess how long she'd stayed awake reliving his kiss, wishing she'd had the courage to agree to his suggestion for making memories.

He rose and began to go down the stairs.

"I heard Rosalie a little while ago," he said.

Nervous, she looked at him from the corner of her eye. He seemed totally content, not a bit disturbed by her refusal last night. Swallowing hard, Caroline hoped desperately that her own demeanor looked as serene.

Once seated with breakfast before them, Caroline looked at him gravely. "Tell me about your company."

He looked at her for a moment, then complied and told her how he'd leveraged his assets until he'd attained controlling interest in the software firm. How he hired local talent from Tulane and some of the other southern universities and how fast it'd expanded. Now it was poised to make another leap forward.

"I can't believe you got the financing initially. It sounds

so scary. What if you hadn't succeeded?" she said at one point.

It sounded complicated, daring and extraordinarily perilous. He had been a brave young man—assured of his abilities and leveraging them to the man he was today.

"Nothing worth achieving's done without some risk. There was a lot involved, but I relished the opportunity. It kept me from thinking about you. It was my chance to move ahead. Without it, I'd still be a long way from my goal."

"If it'd failed—" she began, thinking how much she worried about her own ebb and flow of home sales. Her finances were on a much smaller scale than his.

"If it failed, I knew I'd find a job somewhere. I'd have been in debt for the rest of my life, but that was a price I was willing to pay to take the chance."

And that was a basic difference between them, Caroline thought.

She needed security. Brandon thrived on risk.

She enjoyed seeing the enthusiasm with which he explained things. It gave her a different perspective of the man who was still, technically, her husband.

For a moment her mind wandered. Dare she take a chance and refuse to sign the divorce papers, see if they could build some kind of life together?

Would he even consider such a suggestion?

"So what's on your agenda for today?" she asked. "How long are you planning to stay?"

He frowned for a moment. "Aren't we going to review more of Eugenia's papers? Sort through the rest of your grandmother's files?"

"I went through a box a day last week. There're still quite a few left. But of the ones I looked through, there was nothing further on my father."

"Did you and Michelle make any headway?'

"We did. We went through Eugenia's clothes and jewelry and some personal items. The appraisers finished in her bedroom, so we were able to accomplish a lot."

"Did you tell her about your suspicions?"

"No."

Brandon finished his coffee and pushed back from the table. "Let's finish up with the boxes as quickly as possible."

He carried down the remainder of the boxes in several trips. They worked companionably for several hours.

Just before lunch Caroline heard cars in the driveway. She peered out the window surprised to see two unfamiliar cars parking next to Brandon's.

"Who in the world?" she murmured.

Brandon came to look out the window, then turned to head downstairs.

By the time Caroline reached the foyer, two young women were talking with Brandon.

"What's going on?" Caroline asked.

Three pairs of eyes looked at her.

Brandon spoke first. "Ladies, this is Caroline Madison. Caroline, meet Wendy and Stella. They're here to help us sort."

Caroline blinked and then frowned.

"Could I speak to you, Brandon?" she said calmly, stepping into the room off the foyer.

He followed a couple of seconds later.

"What are they doing here and who are they?" she said in a low voice.

What was he thinking? To broadcast her grandmother's possible indiscretions to the world?

"There's too much to do in a short time. I hired some help. These women are from a temporary agency. With their help, we should be through everything by the end of tomorrow."

"I don't want half the town knowing about this," she hissed.

"Relax, Caroline. One of the guarantees of the agency is discretion. And neither of these women had even heard of your grandmother. They're not reading any more than necessary to sort personal papers and discard the rest. Don't worry, Eugenia's memory will still be sacrosanct."

"I don't care about her memory. It's my family's business I don't want broadcast to all of Baton Rouge."

"It won't be."

"You should've asked me," she said, mollified a little by his assurances.

"Maybe, but you have to admit this is a lot more efficient than only the two of us plowing through everything."

"And costly, I bet. How much?"

"Nothing for you to worry about."

"You're not paying."

"Why not? I hired them. I can afford it. You're worrying about nothing. Accept the help and let's get on with it."

"I suppose we're to feed them," she said, not wanting to

examine how disappointed she was to not have Brandon alone at lunch.

Stepping back, as if to distance herself from her own thoughts, she frowned. She'd succeeded in relegating Brandon to the back of her mind while he was in New Orleans. It wasn't fair now that they had the afternoon together, she had to share him with two strangers.

"Rosalie can feed them on the veranda and you and I can eat inside, if you like," he said easily.

"Well, that's dumb. That'd make more work for Rosalie."

He smiled. "We'll do whatever you wish," he said.

The work went fast, Caroline had to admit later that afternoon. Wendy and Stella were efficient and hardworking. By five o'clock, most of the boxes had been emptied. Only one was still half full.

"I'll sort those tomorrow," Brandon said after the women departed. "You have a different role. You need to read all the correspondence they separated. You know what you're looking for. And as a head start you'll have everything in chronological order."

"What if there's nothing?" she asked, looking without enthusiasm at the stacks of paper.

"You tell me. Can you live with the conviction that she interfered in your parents' lives as she did in ours and somehow caused your father to leave without ever finding the proof?"

"I don't know. It's hard to believe, even after learning what she did between us."

"She was a difficult woman, convinced her way was

right. And ruthless in attempting to make sure everyone conformed to her ideas," he said harshly. "She knew how to play on people's emotions. And your mother must have been a hot bed of emotions being pregnant. Who knows what Eugenia told her or how much she ranted."

"I know."

She closed her eyes, feeling memories of the past press down on her.

"She was a difficult woman to live with. I never met her expectations. Neither did Michelle or Abby. But I don't think it weighed on them as much."

"Because you sheltered them from the full brunt of her personality?" he guessed.

She shivered. "Maybe. I was the oldest. I had to take care of them when Mama died."

"And because you felt guilty your father left."

She shrugged.

That guilt had been relegated to the past. The guilt that plagued Caroline now was her own part in the demise of her marriage. She should have contacted Brandon. She never should have listened to her grandmother.

Why hadn't she trusted herself and the love she once felt for this special man?

She'd give anything for the ability to do it all over.

But there were no do-overs in life.

Rosalie served dinner on the veranda.

Brandon seated Caroline, then sat across from her.

"Do you always eat outside when it's warm?" he asked as they ate the delicious Shrimp Creole the cook had prepared.

"No. Actually, I've only eaten out here since Eugenia's death. She insisted on using the dining room once we were old enough to not spill at every meal."

"And you prefer a less formal setting?"

She nodded, thinking about their apartment. She'd avoided any hint of pretension or elegance. It had been colorful, warm and relaxing. None of the furnishings had matched, but they all went well together. It had been designed for comfort, not for show.

Her condo in Dallas reflected a more mature blending of styles and fabrics, but essentially captured a similar feeling of warmth and comfort rather than the more austere elegance of Talmadge Hall.

"How long are you staying?" Caroline asked after finishing her meal.

Now that he had her consent for the divorce, there was no reason to remain, was there?

Except to make some more memories as he'd suggested. She felt her face grow warm and quickly reached for her glass of iced tea in hopes of hiding the fact.

"In a hurry to see me leave?"

"No, but with all the demands you have, I expect this isn't easy—being here when so many things are happening in New Orleans."

"I can take a day here or there," he said dryly.

For the first time in a long while, Caroline felt content.

When Rosalie brought out Bananas Foster and coffee for dessert, Caroline decided to take each minute as it came.

She and Brandon discussed everything from popular

movies, to books read. Caroline was surprised Brandon indulged in Netflix, but she hid it. She didn't know when he found time to watch anything, but apparently he wasn't totally consumed with work.

When the conversation veered to his parents. Caroline expressed her regret at learning of his father's passing shortly after she last saw him. She heard the sadness in Brandon's voice when he talked about him. He'd succeeded far beyond anything his father achieved, but he'd loved and respected his father and it still showed.

"And your mother's living in Florida now, you said."

"She has a nice condo there. She took some of the furniture she and Dad had and then we bought new things for her new place. We could have used your help in setting her up. But it's nice," he said.

"She's happy there?"

"She loves it. One of her long time friends lives close by. She joined a bridge club and a touring group. Even does Jazzercise. She let me buy the condo and furnish it. I wanted to do more."

Caroline longed to reach out to touch him.

Bitterly angry at her grandmother for robbing her of that right, she clenched her hand into a tight fist.

"They had a happy home. I remember thinking that each time we visited," she said softly.

"But not a lot of material things. They didn't even have a microwave," he said in disbelief.

Caroline laughed. "Your mother loved to cook. The convenience of a microwave would have been lost on her. Things and money aren't necessary to make people happy."

"Easy to say when you've had it all your life."

Caroline started to tell him she'd been totally self-sufficient from the time of their separation until the present, but didn't. It was an old argument, and not one she could change by words.

"Do you miss your old home?" she asked.

"Not particularly. I like New Orleans. Why?"

"I wondered if you did, you seem so surprised we want to sell Talmadge Hall that I thought maybe you might have wished to keep your family's home."

"Mom didn't want to stay there. I certainly never planned to move back. So she sold it and now has a nice nest egg for the future."

"That's what Michelle, Abby and I will have upon the sale of Talmadge Hall. A nice nest egg for the future."

She swallowed hard and fell silent. She didn't want to think about the future tonight. Not while Brandon was still here.

"I can give you a nest egg as a settlement," he said slowly.

She stared at him with horrified eyes.

"No! I don't want anything. You made all that money, risked everything to buy into the company. And did it all after we separated. I'm not entitled to any of it."

"Sure you are. It was acquired while we were married."

"I don't want anything!" she repeated.

"I'd feel better if you took some." He'd done it for her, after all.

"If you keep up talk like that I'll refuse to sign the papers," she threatened.

Chapter Seven

The night sounds were a quiet background to the lazy murmur of the river. Caroline took a sip of the dark chicory coffee, wishing she hadn't brought up the divorce. She wanted to savor the peaceful evening, one of her favorite times of the day. And savor the darkness. It was the best time to talk, share confidences and to draw closer.

She remembered sneaking into her sisters' rooms—sometimes all three of them gathered in one bedroom, against their grandmother's strict rules. The spice of the forbidden only adding to their delight. They'd share dreams and plans for the future, always in the darkness. Abby would curl up against her when she was very young. Michelle always wanted to be on the edge of the bed. Caroline liked being in the middle, as if being surrounded by those she loved could insulate her from the fears and uncertainties that plagued her.

"It's still early," Caroline said when she finished her coffee. "I guess I have time to start reading through those old letters and papers."

"Want any help?"

"No."

She did, but thought it prudent to spend some time alone. She didn't want him to think she couldn't manage things on her own. She'd grown up a lot in the years since they'd been together.

It was only a couple of hours later when the writing began to blur that she wished she'd said yes. His presence in the living room as she read would have kept her company. Now she felt lonely. A common feeling over the last few years, but not one she liked.

Rising, she straightened the two piles, read and unread—the unread still much larger than the other. But Caroline had discovered more about her grandmother. And every speck of information led her to believe more strongly that Eugenia Talmadge had been a ruthless manipulative mean spirited woman—determined to get her own way in everything she wanted.

But there were no new clues about her father.

She switched off the light and wandered out into the foyer. The front door was locked. The rest of the ground floor in darkness. Only the chandelier over the stairs remained on.

Slowly, quietly, she climbed the stairs. Rosalie had departed immediately after supper. Brandon must have closed up the house and gone to bed.

She entered her room and quickly got ready for bed. Opening the wide French doors to the balcony, she looked at the empty expanse. Had she expected him to be there? To sweep her off her feet and carry her away to a world of private delight?

As she slipped into bed and pulled the light sheet over her, Caroline admitted she had.

Late the next morning, Caroline impatiently glanced at the wall clock again—for at least the fifty-third time. Last night Brandon suggested they go out for lunch. She hadn't seen him all morning. And she was having trouble focusing on the old documents when her mind kept wondering where he was.

He hadn't left, his car was still in the drive. He must be in his room. Working probably. She didn't know why she was so antsy. She'd told Rosalie not to make lunch, so she sure hoped he'd been serious when suggesting they go out for lunch.

Once again, she surveyed her piles of papers. There were three now. One to be read, one read and keep and the growing one of read and toss.

The cream and burgundy decor of the room gave the room warmth yet enhanced a feeling of spaciousness. If she separated her feelings from living in the house, she could admit it was a lovely historic old home. Eugenia had been a good owner, keeping up all maintenance and renovations to maintain it as a lovely estate. If only it had been fused with love.

She hoped a large family bought it so the rooms would ring with children laughing and playing and celebrating holidays with love and happiness.

Love was the key ingredient. She wondered if Eugenia'd had any concept of the emotion.

Not for the first time she wondered how Eugenia had

lived with herself after what she'd done first to her mother, then to herself.

She'd never made the attempt to return to New Orleans. She'd believed her grandmother's lies. But still now in retrospect, she knew she could have reached out at least once. She hadn't been thinking clearly, granted. And hearing over and over about how he married her for her money, and never made any effort to contact her, had definitely played a part in her decision.

How could the woman have so blatantly lied? Especially when she saw how depressed Caroline had been.

She was proud of what she'd accomplished since moving out of Talmadge Hall a second time. She was doing well and could provide for herself. She didn't want a settlement from Brandon. Not that she'd need anything after the Talmadge's estate was settled.

Hearing a sound in the hallway, Caroline scrambled to her feet.

"Brandon, I'm in here."

Caroline's face lit up when she saw him. She couldn't help it. For a moment, she felt like the college coed being courted by the man of her dreams.

Ten minutes later they left for lunch. Caroline took them to a small family restaurant that was a favorite of hers. The hostess greeted her by name and showed them immediately to a choice patio table beneath a wide umbrella.

Shaded beside a huge trellis, the patio had a small fountain in the back splashing merrily on rocks. An ornate cage of mourning doves to one side provided a melodious background.

Businessmen and women were seated at tables scattered around the patio.

Once they'd ordered, Caroline turned to him, to ask what he'd done all morning.

"I finished sorting the last box. Not many personal papers in it. I'll bring those down when we get home. Then I had a conference call with some of the team on our problem customer."

"Can you do remote work?"

He nodded. "Sure. We're a high tech firm, we can do a lot remotely. That makes it easier when I travel. Not like your job. You really have to be there, right?"

She nodded. "I have a couple of sales that are closing soon. One of the gals in the office will handle the final paperwork for me if I don't get back in time. Depending on how long the Realtor here thinks it'll take to sell Talmadge Hall, I probably won't stay until it sells. It's such a big property, I doubt it'll move quickly."

She had to wait for the estate to be settled to cut all ties to Baton Rouge. But she knew she'd need patience until it sold.

"So tell me about how you came to start a career in real estate," Brandon suggested.

Caroline complied, forgetting where she was, that others might be eavesdropping on her conversation. Her enthusiasm for her own business was strong and she loved talking about it. Had their baby lived, she knew she'd have been a doting mother. With no child to pour her attention on, business had become her passion.

"Why don't you sell Talmadge Hall? Not list it with another agent," he asked.

"I'm not licensed in Louisiana. Plus, I don't want to hang around long enough for it to sell. I have my life in Dallas."

There were no warm feelings associated with the old house. She wanted to be rid of it and to forget she'd ever lived there.

Brandon looked at his plate. Most of his lunch was finished. He had mixed emotions when she talked about leaving as soon as the house was listed. She was anxious to get back to Dallas.

He remembered when she'd been anxious for him to get home. He remembered her loving arms greeting him each night and her passionate kisses each morning, which almost compelled him to stay home with her all day and forget work.

And he remembered how happy she'd been when she'd discovered she was pregnant.

He'd wanted to give her the moon.

"Tell me about your condo," he said, pushing away the old memories. It was enough today to spend a few more hours with her. Tonight he'd end the idyllic visit, give her the papers to sign and return to New Orleans in the morning.

"It's a few blocks from where I work. If I don't need my car during the day, I usually walk to work. But if I'm showing property, of course I drive."

It was mid afternoon by the time they returned to Talmadge Hall.

"Want something to drink?" she asked when they entered the cool foyer.

"Iced tea sounds good. How about you?"

"Yes. I know Rosalie keeps a pitcher in the refrigerator. I'll be right back."

Brandon went into the large living room. He wandered around the spacious room studying the paintings, the knickknacks that Eugenia'd scattered around—a porcelain figure on a side table, a glass globe with a flower forever suspended inside on the bookshelves against the far wall. Limoge porcelain boxes, a Faberge egg. A framed picture of Caroline with her sisters. That was unexpected. He picked it up, remembering the day it was taken. Both Michelle and Abby had come to New Orleans right after school that June. They'd all gone to the French Quarter, acting like tourists, pigging out with beignets at the Café du Monde, wandering through the Quarter, listening to jazz. He'd snapped the shot with Abby's camera.

They all looked so happy.

And so young.

Replacing it gently, he realized that was another aspect of Caroline forever lost.

Today the hint of sadness in her eyes, the pensive moods she sometimes fell into, were all changes the years and circumstances had wrought. She no longer looked young and carefree.

"Here's the tea," Caroline said, coming into the room and handing Brandon a tall glass.

I noticed the answering machine blinking when I passed

the office, I'm going to listen to the messages."

Brandon followed her to the office, noting the blinking light.

"Hey Caroline, I haven't heard from you in a while, kiddo. Your cell went to voice mail, too. Call me."

Another beep, then a strong masculine voice, came on,

"Caroline? Dennis here. Where are you? I've tried calling your cell, but no response from there. Trying here now. I am happy to offer my services if you need any help with the estate. Do give me a call."

Another beep, then silence.

"Who is Dennis?" Brandon asked.

Caroline looked at him in some surprise. "A friend."

He stepped closer and unfolded his arms.

"Was that Susan Carmody?" he asked.

She nodded. "Though she's married now and it's Susan Andrews. But yes. I'm surprised you remembered her."

"You and she were friends since first grade, why wouldn't I remember that?"

"You only met her once. We weren't married long enough for us to spend much time with any of my friends."

"Who is Dennis?" he asked again. "How good a friend?" A hard edge colored his voice.

She shook her head, and looked him in the eye. "Not that it's any of your business, Dennis is just a friend. Nothing more."

"It's my business until you sign those divorce papers," he said, reaching out to cradle her head in his large hands. "Until then, you're still my wife." Lowering his face he started to kiss her, but Caroline pulled away.

"Stop, Brandon. What we had is over. I can have whomever I wish to have as a friend. Did you think I lived in a vacuum since you've been gone?"

"Who left who, sweetheart?" he asked, a dangerous glint in his eyes.

She took a breath and nodded her head. "Okay, so maybe technically I left you. And with grandmother's interference we never got back together. But I wrote you. About six weeks later I did write. It was just before I went to see Jodi. In fact, not hearing back solidified my plans to visit her."

She sighed and bit her lower lip. "I take it the letter never reached you?"

He shook his head. "Why didn't you just come to New Orleans?" he asked.

"Because I hadn't heard anything from you and I thought you didn't care. I did call the apartment. No answer. When I called a few weeks later, the phone had been disconnected."

He nodded. "A few weeks after you left, I got a cell phone and canceled the land line. I'd given up hope of hearing from you by then."

She nodded, thinking suddenly that if they'd both had cell phones five years ago calls couldn't have been intercepted.

"By then I couldn't stay at the Hall any longer. She was driving me crazy. Michelle had found a job in New Orleans and Abby graduated from high school and seemed set on nursing. I wanted some plan in my life, some goal or purpose. The plans we made were in ashes. So I thought if we talked—I don't know, maybe I could get a clue about what I needed to do with the rest of my life."

"I never knew," he said.

"I guessed as much the other day. At the time she said it was further proof that you really had no use for me and I should cut my losses. She sounded sympathetic. Now of course I know it for the lie it was."

"So I'm here now. We're face-to-face. Maybe it's time to talk things out. See what we want to do from this point forward."

"I thought you wanted to end things once and for all."

"I need to change the status quo, Caroline. Either end the marriage or resume it."

She stared at him. He'd voiced what she'd been thinking about for days. Was it possible for them to resume it?

Why the sudden change of heart?

"Resume it? Didn't we just agree to a divorce!"

"It's been at the back of my mind since we made love. I think we should at least discuss it."

"I have my business in Dallas, you live in New Orleans where your company is. I don't see how we can make that work."

"I didn't say it'll be easy, necessarily. But it's an option to consider. Or we can continue with the divorce proceedings."

He said it as if both choice held the same appeal.

Which would he prefer? she wondered.

"I don't know."

Did she wish to change things? They couldn't go back. Did she wish to open herself up to the uncertainty of living with Brandon again? Of trying to make a strong marriage on the ashes of their first attempt?

"Come down and visit this weekend and see how you like it. It's been a while since you were there," he suggested.

"Five years. I've never been back."

"Come for the weekend. At the very least you can give me some pointers on my apartment. It doesn't give me a welcoming vibe like our place did. I think you could change that."

Caroline was tempted. What'd one weekend hurt? Especially if it led to a reconciliation?

No, not a reconciliation—not in the truest sense of the word. Just a resumption of their marriage.

No, not quite that, either.

Maybe seeing Brandon in his own space, seeing how he lived now would help. Was it wishful thinking, or was there a possibility—no matter how slight—that things might work?

"I can't come this weekend. I have the appraisers coming again and a real estate agent. I don't want to put them off."

"Next weekend, then."

Feeling a curl of anticipation, Caroline slowly nodded. "Okay, next weekend."

"Come on Friday."

"If I do, I expect you to be there when I'm there, Brandon. Not working late, no dashing off for a quick minute on Saturday that turns into an all day event."

Slowly he smiled, his eyes warming as he gazed down into hers. Caroline felt her heart turn somersaults.

No other man had ever captivated her as Brandon. Nor had any enticed her beyond a friendly meal or a visit to the local movie theater. Brandon had outright spoiled her for other men. His smile had the power to melt her bones, his touch wreaked havoc with her senses and his voice could charm the birds from the trees.

"If we are even beginning to explore resuming our marriage, I don't think you should be seeing anyone else," he said.

"I'm not seeing anyone," she replied taking another sip of her iced tea.

He glanced at the answering machine.

She signed in exasperation. "Dennis was a friend of my grandmother's. He's in his late fifties. I hardly think you need to feel any competition with him," she said dryly.

Brandon drained the glass and handed it to her.

"I have to be heading out. I want to be back in the office this afternoon before it closes. See you a week from Friday."

He was almost to the front door before she could speak.

"Wait! What do you mean? You're leaving now?"

She followed him, watching in disbelief .

"I have work to do." His hand on the doorknob, he looked at her. "If you can get there by lunchtime, let me know. We'll have lunch together. Otherwise, I'll plan on dinner next Friday."

"I don't know where you live or work," she said, trying to prolong his stay. His leaving caught her totally unaware.

Reaching into his inside pocket he withdrew a card and handed it to her, careful to keep his fingers from touching her.

Caroline looked at it and then Brandon.

What was going on? He'd invited her to visit and once she said yes, he couldn't get away fast enough?

What about his suggestion they consider trying again?

"I'll see you a week from Friday."

He left before she could say another word.

"Blast it!"

The man was the most confusing person she knew. And the most infuriating. She'd thought he'd spend the week. Stupid of her to assume that. He'd never said how long he planned to stay.

That showed her that figuring out things was far from a sure thing.

The next morning Caroline dressed conservatively for her meeting with the attorney. She hadn't told Brandon about the appointment. Of course she had other things to think about. Mostly how she felt about him and if being with him a few hours here and there were enough to consider his suggestion of giving their marriage another try.

She'd have liked something a bit more romantic, something to give her an indication of how he felt about things—especially as it hadn't been that long since they'd agreed to a divorce.

She'd lost so much more than a baby and husband five years ago. She'd lost the ability to believe in happy-ever-after, to believe love lasted.

She paused on her way out of the old mansion to glare at Eugenia's portrait over the mantel in the living room. She knew now that Brandon hadn't been the irresponsible, uninterested, self-serving man Eugenia made him out to be. He'd tried to contact her, but Eugenia had interfered.

Just as she'd done twenty years earlier.

More than ever Caroline wanted to find out the truth about her father. Something to give her the closure she needed. Just to know he'd not willingly walked away from his wife and daughters would make a world of difference to her.

Time enough later to dwell on that. Right now she had to hurry or risk being late.

An hour and a half later Caroline stepped outside the lawyer's office into the sunlight, shocked. Being late would have been the least of her problems, she thought as she checked her watch.

She began walking slowly back to her car, feeling totally confused. There was almost too much to comprehend, she thought dazed. Too much to calmly return home and act as if her entire world hadn't been turned upside down yet again.

She tossed the thick envelope with the copies of the papers the attorney had reviewed onto the front seat. She needed to tell Michelle and Abby. They were both counting on money from the estate.

How would they react when she told them there was nothing but debts?

She needed to see them in person; this was not something she wanted to share over the phone.

They could meet when she went to New Orleans. She'd call and tell them she was coming and arrange a convenient time for them to get together.

Leaning her head against her seat back, she closed her eyes. Tired beyond belief, she wished fervently for an end to it all. The revelations kept coming and coming and she wasn't sure she was up to dealing with them. Opening her eyes, she took a deep breath. She'd have to be.

She wasn't looking forward to telling her sisters there was no money. Just thinking about explaining how Eugenia had incurred monumental debts just to keep that monstrous house of hers going infuriated her.

She sure didn't want Brandon finding out either. Not yet anyway.

Would he see her tentative exploration of getting back together a way to insure she had money? She'd wished now she'd told him about the attorney's visit. Actually, she really wished he'd come with her.

She refused to let him think she was a gold digger.

Instead of thinking about getting back together, she now wondered if her best course would be go through with the divorce.

What was she going to do?

Chapter Eight

The week dragged by for Caroline. After meeting with the appraisers and the realtor and continuing to read through the papers her grandmother had left, Caroline was more than ready for a break.

Instead, she had more papers to read through in an attempt to find incontrovertible proof her grandmother had been instrumental in driving their father away. She wondered how much more she needed. After learning how Eugenia had sabotaged her own marriage, Caroline had no doubts about her parents' breakup.

Still she was burning with curiosity.

She wondered if she could locate Edith. The woman obviously knew what happened.

Caroline didn't remember anyone named Edith visiting her grandmother through the years. Had their friendship lasted beyond that scathing letter?

When Brandon called on Wednesday evening, she was surprised how happy she was to hear his voice.

"We're still on for Friday, right?"

"Yes. I'm looking forward to it. I'm so tired of all the decisions I have to make with regard to the estate. The appraiser recommended different vendors to sell everything. Calling and arranging for each of them to come by to see if they would in fact like to take the furniture or art took a couple of days to set up. Then I've had people traipsing through the house at all hours. I can't wait to get away."

"We'll do only fun things when you're here."

"I do need to see my sisters," she said. She still had that ahead of her.

"How are you doing getting through your grandmother's papers?" he asked.

"I've read everything up to seven years ago. It's going fast now. I doubt there'll be any mention of it after all this time. I did find an envelope with my mother's death certificate and each of our birth certificates."

"Did you know when your mother died?"

"Yes. We've always known that from visiting her grave. It was funny to see the birth certificates, though. Sam Williams is our father's name, you know. But we've always used Talmadge," she said slowly.

"How did that happen?"

"Apparently Mama took it back after he left. I don't even remember being called Williams, but then I was so little when it all happened. I haven't found anything to show that the names were legally changed—my name and Michelle's and Abby's. Do you suppose that makes our marriage illegal?"

"No, it doesn't." His tone was sharp, forceful.

"It might be a moot point, I guess."

"Because?"

"If we decide to divorce."

"We'll talk about that on the weekend. What time are you coming?"

"I'll try to be there for lunch."

"I'll arrange to be free."

"Okay. And I really need to meet my sisters for lunch on Saturday. It's the only time Abby had available. So, if you have something to do then—"

She hated to bring up the lunch, but after making such a point of wanting him to spend time with her exclusively, she needed to let him know she couldn't reciprocate.

"I'm not invited, eh?"

How could she tactfully explain? She wouldn't invite him even if she didn't have bad news to share. She didn't want to give rise to any speculation from her sisters before she and Brandon's plans were final—whichever way they went.

"It's a girls' lunch."

"Save dinner for me, then."

"I will."

She hung up, still unsure of her feelings. Impatient to see him again, reluctant to be drawn closer, she wasn't sure what she expected or wanted. Only, she was sure she'd go through with the visit.

She had to know what the future might hold.

By Friday, Caroline was a nervous wreck. She'd packed and unpacked four times, trying to choose just the right clothes. She wanted to show Brandon how far she'd come from the young college girl who'd rebelled against her formal, regal grandmother. Her casual clothes now carried the look of distinction. No more jeans with the knees torn. Instead she had slacks and shirts that fit her slender frame and displayed her womanly attributes. Discreet jewelry. For dinner, she'd chosen a silk dress in dark blue. With a plunging neckline and close-fitting bodice, it also made her feel very sexy.

She shook her head. She was not trying to seduce him. She and Brandon needed to sit down and have a frank discussion about what they each wanted, what they each expected if they tried again. The fact she was even thinking about it still astonished her.

By late Friday morning, Caroline felt like a wire being drawn tighter and tighter. The closer she drove toward New Orleans, the more her emotions began to change. Trepidation filled her.

She wanted to see Brandon, and her sisters, but was she ready to face New Orleans? She'd been so happy there and so devastated. Memories sprang to mind, lingered. The university, nights studying while Brandon worked beside her. Decorating their apartment on a shoestring budget. The walks she and Brandon took along the Mississippi. Shopping for Christmas gifts. They'd only had one Christmas together.

Finally she let the memories of their excitement over the baby come to the surface. She'd been thrilled about their coming child. As had Brandon.

Once again, she savored the memory of his pleasure in the first teddy bear they bought right after they confirmed she was pregnant. He'd wanted to buy a football, but she'd asked him to wait until they at least knew if the baby was a boy or girl.

She remembered what he said about turning to work to fill the emptiness left by their loss.

She'd been too young to articulate her needs. She'd expected him to intuitively know she ached with sorrow and make things better for her. But she'd never realized he'd felt the same way. That he'd needed comfort and reassurance, too.

Was she more mature now? Could she deal better with the vagaries of fate in the future because of the past?

She sure hoped so.

The traffic grew heavier, demanding her attention. The old memories were once again relegated to another time.

Weaving around the area near Canal Street, she located the high-rise in which Brandon's company was housed. Parking was a problem, but she finally found a spot. Checking her watch, she saw it was not quite noon.

She entered the cavernous lobby and located the building directory. His offices were on the twelfth floor. She headed for the elevators and in only a minute she stepped into the tastefully decorated lobby.

"May I help you?" The receptionist behind the desk was pretty, blond and young and a perfect image for an up and coming software firm.

"I'm here to see Brandon Madison," Caroline said with a smile.

"Is he expecting you?"

"Yes."

"Whom shall I say?"

"His wife." She couldn't help the pride in her voice.

Caroline hadn't said the words aloud in years.

But they felt right.

Was she already committed to making an attempt to restart their marriage?

Or was it for the sheer pleasure of seeing the woman's eyes widen, her expression change.

Before the receptionist could notify Brandon, he strode into the lobby from the hall to the left.

"Caroline," he said.

An imp of mischief, spurred from the receptionist's surprise, had Caroline reach up and offer a kiss.

"Hello, darling."

"I see you got here safely," he said, not by a flicker of his expression showing any surprise at her greeting.

She tucked her hand into his arm and smiled up at him.

"Of course, though I'd forgotten how awful the traffic is in this city. Do we have time for you to show me around?"

He nodded and started back down the hall.

"Care to share with me what game you're playing now?" he asked once they were out of the reception area.

She looked up at him with feigned innocence. "Why, Brandon, no games. Can't a wife greet her husband?"

"Right."

He walked straight through his secretary's area without saying a word—even when the woman looked up expectantly. Pulling Caroline into his office, he shut the door, leaned against it and pulled her into his arms. His kiss was all she remembered—hot and exciting.

Forgetting everything but the pleasure his kiss brought,

she wondered if they could skip lunch?

Brandon deepened the kiss. One touch of her mouth against his and he forgot everything except the feel of Caroline in his arms. Her slim body was pressed against his. He could feel her soft curves. Her arms were tight around his neck and she returned his kiss fervently.

When he finally eased away to look down at her, she raised her lids and gazed back. He noted she was breathless and smiled suddenly. Past and present mingled. But was he opening himself up for future heartache? He had his life as he wanted it. Work was compelling and satisfying. He had a small circle of friends.

Yet he'd missed this woman like no one else in his life.

His attorney thought him a fool to pursue this chancy arrangement, but he was in for the long haul—to see what they could salvage, if anything, from their marriage.

"Wow," she said, a smile lighting her eyes. "Another memory?"

He looked ruefully around his office. Another memory? From when he'd suggested they make memories to last forever. One he'd regret if they didn't try again. His office had been safe from reminders of Caroline before this. Now he'd remember this moment, this kiss for a long time.

"I've missed you. Are you ready for lunch?" he asked, taking a step away. His hands lingering a moment longer than necessary as if he couldn't let her go.

He was ready for a lot more than eating, but knew the value of patience in delicate negotiations.

So much had changed in the last few weeks, he could

afford to wait and see what developed. If things weren't going the way he wanted, he'd try a different tactic.

"Yes, I'm hungry," she said. "But show me around first, please. In case we don't make it back today."

He tried to guess what she meant, but the only thought he had was of them going back to his apartment when lunch was over and definitely not returning to work today.

"We'll have a quick tour. There's not much to see. Programmers working on computers."

"Are you free the rest of the day?"

"Yes."

He crossed to the desk and closed a folder, tidied a stack of papers. Looking up at her, he winked.

"Free all weekend. We'll do whatever tourists in New Orleans like."

"I'm hardly a tourist," she said, walking over to the window to look out at the view. His office was near Canal Street, not too far from the Quarter. Beyond the French Quarter she could glimpse a swath of the Mississippi River. Container ships were inching by the Crescent City, on their way to sea.

It felt strange to be back. Surreal.

"Where are you parked?" Brandon asked.

"About two blocks over. I'll have to move the car. It's in a two-hour limit."

"Give me the keys, I'll have someone drive it to my place."

She smiled and reached into her purse for the keys.

Things had definitely changed. What an extravagance.

"And how will that person return to work?"

"Get a Uber or a cab. How should I know?" he asked impatiently.

"Nice to be a boss," she murmured with a smile.

"It is," he affirmed.

He gave her a whirlwind tour of the office, introducing her to his secretary, to project leads and programmers. Then they ate lunch at a small bistro off Canal Street. Brandon suggested they change their clothes into more casual wear before prowling around the Quarter. Despite the time of year, it was hot in New Orleans.

He flagged a cab and in only moments they were in the renovated district near the River. The old warehouses had been converted to expensive apartments and condominiums. He opened the door to his building and escorted Caroline to the elevator, wondering what she'd think about his place. It was a far cry from their little apartment near the university.

He opened the door and stood aside for her to enter, wishing he could be privy to her thoughts when she first saw it.

Caroline stepped inside and looked around. Sleek, sophisticated and cold were the first three adjectives that came to mind. Dismayed, she kept walking into the room, afraid to let Brandon see her expression.

Was this the kind of home he liked? He must have hated their place with the vibrant colors and clutter. She liked pillows and plants and pictures and color above all. This room looked like a museum or showcase.

"It's nice," she said when the silence stretched out

awkwardly. She spotted her suitcases with her keys on top. "If you tell me where to change, I'll only be a minute."

He closed the door and walked over, turning her around and raising her face with a finger.

"Where do you want to stay, Caroline? My room or the guest room?"

She frowned, wishing he'd made that decision.

"The guest room," she said at last.

Nothing had been settled. She needed some space before committing herself. There was still a lot to decide. And so much to work through before she'd feel truly comfortable around Brandon.

If he were disappointed, he hid it . Lifting her bags, he led the way.

"Follow me" was all he said.

Alone a few seconds later, Caroline unpacked and surveyed the clothes she'd brought. Deciding on a casual skirt and cool lacy top, she quickly changed. Brushing her hair, she checked in the mirror. Ready as I'll ever be, she thought.

When she walked into the living room Brandon stood by the window, talking on the phone. He turned and beckoned her over.

"I can be there for a while tomorrow, one o'clock. But I won't stay long."

Caroline stepped into his arm as naturally as if she'd been doing it for years, instead of having a long gap when they'd been apart. She breathed in his subtle scent, looking out across the Mississippi, and wondering if she was doing the right thing by coming to New Orleans. Too late now to have second thoughts. At least she wasn't bombarded with memories of her loss. She was taking one day at a time.

She refused to allow her doubts to take hold.

He hung up the phone and kissed her cheek gently. "All set?"

"Business again?" she asked.

"Right. But this weekend's for you. Since you're having lunch tomorrow with your sisters, I'll meet with Patterson then, and be free by the time you are."

"Fair enough. Where to first?"

"Jax? Then we can wander around the Quarter, have an afternoon snack at the Cafe du Monde."

"You must think I really am a tourist."

"Sturdy walking shoes?" he asked, checking.

"Comfortable and enduring."

He took her hand, threading his fingers through hers. "Let's go play tourist."

Caroline's memories again mingled with the present, remembering Brandon's likes and dislikes as easily as she knew her own. They'd often walked around the French Quarter when younger, an inexpensive way to spend a lazy Sunday or to hunt bargains for their apartment.

It was as if they'd never been apart.

Yet once in a while, Brandon seemed like a stranger. It was disconcerting, but Caroline was determined to explore all facets of the man beside her. This weekend could be the most important one of her life.

They wandered around the Quarter, stopped in shops,

watched sidewalk artists sketch other tourists. Refusing a carriage ride, they darted across the street from Jackson Square to snack on beignets and café au lait.

They ate dinner at a Cajun place on a side street, then walked back through the twilight to Brandon's apartment.

When Brandon switched on the light in the living room, he looked around and frowned. This place wasn't welcoming at all. Whatever they decided about their future, he wanted Caroline to do something with his home.

"What do you think about the apartment?" he asked.

"It's nice."

"It's not like our place was. When I first got it, I wanted something very different. Now, I don't know."

He shook his head and headed for the kitchen.

"Want something to drink?"

"Iced tea."

She looked at the room from a professional perspective. If she were going to list this place, she'd stage it to be lots more homey.

"It needs some color," she called.

She wanted to see the rest of the apartment beyond the guest room. Following him into the kitchen, she noted the stainless-steel appliances, the austere counter space. A modern kitchen helped sell homes. A sterile one looked like a hospital.

"It also doesn't look as if anyone lives here," she said slowly.

Brandon shrugged. "I've lived here for years. I had a professional design the place."

He looked up from pouring iced tea from a pitcher and caught her eye. "Want to have a go at it?"

"What would you like?"

"Whatever you like, I'm sure will suit me. Make it like the place we had before."

She nodded, ideas already crowding her mind on how to change the austere look into one of warmth and comfort— without making too many alterations or costing him much money.

They drank iced tea sitting side by side on the easy chairs that faced the wide windows, watching the night lights across the river and the slowly moving lights on the riverboats.

It was peaceful, Caroline realized a few minutes later. Not like sitting on the veranda at her grandmother's home. But time for doing that was growing short. Once the house sold, they'd never sit on the veranda again.

They talked about New Orleans, how the Saints were doing, reclamation projects dredging the river and the changes in the Quarter.

When it was completely dark, Brandon took her glass and put it on the table beside his, pulling her into his lap.

"Time to talk about us, Caroline," he said.

She lay against his chest, her eyes still fixed on the darkness outside the apartment. He hadn't turned on any lights, so they were cocooned in the night. Only the lights outside offering a break in the velvety blackness.

She was silent for a long moment, relishing being with Brandon, feeling quietly content for the first time in years.

"I missed you these two weeks," she said slowly, willing

to admit that much, but not more until she had a better feeling of where this conversation was heading. Did he still want to start again?

"That's encouraging," he said dryly.

"I was looking for something more than that in return," she said with spirit.

"What, that I missed you, too? Take it as a given."

"You could have called."

"I did earlier in the week, remember?"

"And the cell towers were down before that?"

"Phones work both ways, Caroline. You could have called me."

He was right. If they were serious about trying again, she needed to do more than sit back and let him pursue her. She'd grown up during the last few years. Everything didn't come automatically. Marriage needed to be a partnership with both partners contributing equally.

"You're right, I should have called," she said. "Especially when I really needed to talk to someone—"

She stopped abruptly, remembering she didn't want to tell Brandon about the news she'd received from the attorney. Time enough once she and her sisters decided on a plan. For now, she'd do her best to keep the weekend pleasant.

"If we decide to restart our marriage, I think we need to discuss ground rules. Make sure our expectations are laid out so there are no surprises and no disappointments," he said slowly.

Caroline realized he'd said nothing about love. Did that

come into the equation? Or had he lost what love he felt for her? Was this an expedient way to end the loneliness they both felt?

"What would you expect?" she asked, almost afraid to hear what he had to say.

His hand rubbed against her arm, his fingers tracing light patterns against her skin. For a moment, she wanted to deny the need for a discussion, turn in his arms and kiss him, have passion take over and block all thoughts and feelings and uncertainties that churned within her.

But Brandon was right. If they wanted a chance at living together again, they needed to be clear about what they expected. This time they'd do best to be up front and honest with each other.

"I'd want to live together," he said.

She nodded, her head brushing against his. "Of course."

Instantly, a million questions surfaced. What about her career? She'd built up a good clientele in Dallas. Moving to New Orleans meant starting over.

"Does that prove a problem?"

"It could. I'd be starting over in an area I'm not familiar with." Just thinking of the challenges ahead had her head swimming.

She knew a long-distance relationship wouldn't work for the long term. Dallas was too far from New Orleans to find a compromise.

Something to consider.

"What about you, will you have to work as long each day now that you've built up your company?" she asked.

"I won't kid you, Caroline, there're a lot of demands on my time. And I love dealing with every aspect. But I'll curtail some of them, find someone else who can handle some of the things I've done. I'll do my best to be home for dinner every night and on the weekends."

"What else?" she asked.

"Children."

She drew in a sharp breath.

"I don't think so, Brandon. I don't want to go through that again. I couldn't bear it."

Tears threatened. Just thinking about how happy they'd been and then the sudden loss was almost more than she could bear.

"We both wanted children before," he said softly. "I still want them. One or two. Someone to leave all that I've built to. You'll be an excellent mother."

Struggling to get up, Caroline pushed out of his lap and moved to the window, leaning against the cool pane. Would this be a deal breaker?

"If that's one of your conditions to resuming this marriage, then we'd better call a halt now. I can't go through that again."

"Another pregnancy doesn't mean you'll miscarry," he said, coming up behind her.

"But I could. I could," she whispered, feeling the familiar ache taking over.

She had yearned for her baby so much, been crushed when she miscarried.

She wasn't strong enough to face that twice in one lifetime.

Chapter Nine

Caroline awoke early the next morning to the aroma of freshly brewing coffee. She turned over in the guest bed and gazed around the room. The decor cried out for as much attention as the living room did. Almost snow-white— everything went together perfectly, yet had no color, no personality, no soul.

She wondered who the interior decorator had been. Either totally into the modern scene, or thinking because Brandon was a guy this is what he'd like.

Stretching slowly, Caroline sat up, the lacy confection of her gown wasted, she thought ruefully.

Brandon hadn't swept her away after the discussion last night. Now it seemed as if they were further from resolving their situation than ever. He wanted children. She couldn't risk it without a built-in guarantee, which she knew life didn't give.

Sighing softly, she worried she'd made a mistake in coming, in considering Brandon's tantalizing suggestion.

She pushed away the sheets and rose. The sky was clear blue, the sun peeping over the horizon. She had lots of time before meeting her sisters. Taking a quick shower, she donned one of the lightweight dresses she'd brought. Sandals on her feet would suffice. She didn't plan on a long walking tour today. And she was anxious to see Brandon. To spend time together and see what resulted.

When she entered the kitchen, Brandon sat at the breakfast nook reading a paper, a half full cup of coffee before him on the table. It looked so ordinary.

But the rapid increase in her heart rate wasn't ordinary— except around Brandon.

For a moment, Caroline wanted to lean over and kiss him to start the day.

Instead she smiled, and said, "Good morning."

He looked up, his eyes gleaming at the sight of her.

"Sleep well?" he asked.

She shrugged. "Not particularly, but not because of the bed."

"Because you really wanted to be in with me, right?" he teased, rising to fetch another cup and pour her coffee.

She wondered how long she could avoid answering that loaded question.

He tilted her face up to his on the way back to the table and brushed his lips across hers. "Well?" he asked, his eyes dancing in amusement.

"Maybe," she admitted grudgingly. She wanted to be honest if they were to make changes.

He almost laughed. "No maybe about it. But we have time. In the interim, what would you like for breakfast?"

"You're going to fix it?" she asked.

"I will if you want, but I was rather hoping you'd insist

on doing the honors. It's been years since I enjoyed your cooking."

"I could make an omelet," she offered.

She remembered exactly how he liked his. In fact, Caroline realized, she remembered everything about Brandon—the Brandon she used to know and love.

That same love that seemed to grow with each passing day.

Startled to admit to herself she still loved him, she moved away, lest she blurt it out.

He'd made no mention of love even when suggesting they restart their marriage—more like offered a renewed partnership.

Was a half loaf better than none? If they resumed their relationship, would he come to fall in love with her again or had her desertion put an end to that forever?

She wasn't sure she wanted a one-sided arrangement. She wanted to be loved. She realized that since her mother died and her marriage ended, she'd felt lost and alone. She knew her sisters loved her, but it wasn't the same.

"If I cook today, are you cooking tomorrow?" she asked, opening cupboard doors hunting for bowls and pans.

"Nope, I thought tomorrow morning we'd get the Sunday paper and head for Café du Monde where we can sip café au lait with beignets and while away the morning reading the paper."

She smiled. That'd been a tradition for them each Sunday. She thought their brief stop there yesterday afternoon had been for old time's sake. Now she was touched he remembered, and seemed to be doing his best to recapture the delightful aspects of their life together.

Only on the question of children were they at different ends of the spectrum.

"When and where are you meeting Abby and Michelle?" Brandon asked as they ate.

"Court of the Two Sisters at twelve-thirty."

She'd chosen that restaurant because of the wide spacing of tables. They'd be assured a certain amount of privacy while talking. They could have met at Michelle's apartment, but Caroline wanted to treat her sisters to lunch. As a kind of celebration of her possible return to New Orleans. Not that she was ready to share that with them yet.

"I'll drop you off on my way to the office. I can pick you up later, if you like," he said easily.

"Not necessary. One of my sisters can drop me back here. Or I'll get a cab. Or even walk if it isn't too hot."

Brandon rose and left, returning in only a moment. "Here. If you get back before I do." He held out a key. By its shiny condition, it looked new.

Caroline stared at it for a long moment. Should she accept?

He took her hand, dropped the key in her palm and closed her fingers over it. His warm hand engulfed hers. She looked up, a question in her eyes.

"No strings," he said.

Did he read minds now? she wondered. When they lived together, he'd seemed completely baffled by her behavior many times. That came from both of them being so young, she thought, so young and untried.

Now he seemed to understand her better. Or was that wishful thinking?

Nodding, she slipped the key into her pocket. "I won't lose it."

"Have you thought about redecorating this place?" he asked as he resumed his seat.

Hesitantly at first, then with more confidence, Caroline told him her ideas for the different rooms she'd seen. By primarily using accessories in bold colors and a few additional pieces of wooden furniture, she could make the apartment into a warm and beautiful home.

Brandon rocked back on the rear legs of his chair. He watched her enthusiasm, nodding from time to time. "Sounds like a plan. Run with it," he said at last.

"I haven't seen the entire apartment."

"Then come on. I'll show you every nook and cranny."

Leaving the dishes on the table, Caroline rose and followed Brandon. She'd seen the guest room and the main bath—it was only his bedroom and attached bath she hadn't seen. He walked into the spacious room then turned and placed his hands on her shoulders.

"My bedroom." He lowered his head and kissed her lightly. "Our room?" he asked softly.

She swallowed and stepped away to study the room. The unmade bed had a dark spread and navy sheets, It looked functional and masculine. She had flower sheets and a comforter with lots of ruffles on her bed. The contrast was interesting to say the least. Somehow she couldn't envision

Brandon sleeping on ruffly, flowered, pastel sheets.

"What do you think?" he asked.

"This room really reflects you," she said. "It's got your stamp on it. The rest of the place looks like no one's at home."

Books were stacked on the bedside table. Change and keys littered the dresser. A large framed photograph of his parents stood in a prominent place.

She looked quickly away.

What had she expected? That he'd have a picture of her in his room?

As far as he'd known, she'd deserted him, relaying the message that she never wanted to see him again. Only an idiot would have kept a picture of someone who'd deserted him.

Anger at her grandmother boiled anew. Caroline wished she'd known. So much time wasted.

"Well?" he prodded.

"Off the top of my head, you don't need much of anything in here," she said. "This room fits you. Maybe some curtains to soften the window. An antique dresser instead of that totally modern one. I think the room would look cozy and inviting."

"Would you be comfortable sleeping in here?"

Heat washed through her. Slowly she envisioned staying with Brandon. Sleeping and waking up with him every day. She almost trembled with sudden longing. She'd missed him so much. It was so unfair what Eugenia had done.

Yet some of the blame fell on her. She shouldn't have

left five years ago. She shouldn't have stayed away once the worst of her pain had faded. She'd failed their marriage, not Brandon.

Slowly, as if reading her mind again, Brandon turned her around and locked her in his arms.

"Want to test the bed?" he asked in a husky voice.

Before she could respond, he lowered his head and kissed her. All thoughts of redecorating fled.

Caroline was late arriving at the Court of the Two Sisters. Both Abby and Michelle were waiting at a table in the courtyard when she arrived. She hurried to join them.

"Sorry. Have you been here long?" she asked, slipping into the empty chair.

"No." Abby said, looking critically at her older sister. She exchanged glances with Michelle. "What have you been up to?" she asked suspiciously.

Caroline blushed and both her sisters grinned.

"As if we didn't know," Michelle said.

"Staying with Brandon, right?" Abby asked.

Caroline picked up her menu and opened it, nodding once in response, trying to hide from their knowing eyes.

Michelle reached out and pushed the menu down. "So what is up? Are the two of you going to become an item again? Or is this just a weekend fling?"

"You don't have flings with your husband," Caroline said primly, wishing she knew how to answer. There was so much to decide. And it all seemed to rest with her.

"It could be when you haven't seen him in five years. What's the scoop?" Abby asked.

She hesitated, then shrugged. They'd find out soon enough.

"Actually, after spending a few days together at Talmadge Hall, we've sort of discussed seeing if we can pick up the threads of our marriage."

"Is this why we're here? To celebrate some momentous change in your life-style?" Abby asked with a big grin.

Caroline shook her head. "Nothing's been decided. Actually, when Brandon came to see me a few weeks ago, it was to ask for a divorce."

"Divorce!" Michelle said.

"Yes."

"Why? After all these years?"

"He can't have found someone new if you are discussing your marriage," Abby said shrewdly.

"No, it was just—closure, I guess you'd say. To do something to change the status quo after so many years."

"How are you doing now that you're here?" Michelle asked.

Both her sisters knew how she equated New Orleans with the saddest time of her life. She hadn't returned since she lost the baby.

"It is easier than you thought, isn't it?" Abby asked.

Caroline nodded. "I guess. That old saying that time heals all wounds is true. I'm still sad, but not like I thought I'd be."

She smiled at her sisters, trying to reassure them.

The old ache would always be with her, but it was getting easier to go on.

"If you do get back with Brandon, you should have another baby right away," Abby said, opening her menu.

"No." Caroline said sharply. "I don't want to go through that again."

Both women stared at her in surprise.

"Just because you had one miscarriage, doesn't mean you'll have another one. I bet you and Brandon would produce some beautiful babies. I remember how excited you were when you discovered you were pregnant before. I can't imagine you not wanting a baby. Or two."

"I don't want to take the risk. Not ever," she said slowly.

She could tell from the look on their faces they didn't understand. Maybe only another woman who had lived through such heartache would understand. She knew she didn't have it in her to try again. Yes, she might carry a baby to term, but she could also lose it and that she couldn't bear.

"However, all this is not why I wanted to see you for lunch. Brandon and I'll have to decide what we want to do. When we do, you two will be the first to know. But in the meantime, I have bad news about Eugenia's estate."

The waitress chose that moment to appear to take their orders. Once she was gone, Michelle turned to Caroline. "Okay, give. What's wrong?"

"There's no money," Caroline said bluntly.

"What?" Abby asked in disbelief. "How can there be no money? Grandmother lived lavishly. She belonged to the country club, had that huge old home with servants, always dressed to the nines. A new outfit every time she had a special event to attend. Donations to charities."

Caroline nodded. "All on borrowed money. It turns out she made some bad investments a number of years ago. She mortgaged Talmadge Hall, then made some more bad investments. Did you ever wonder why she fired the live-in servants? Let the gardener go and made do with someone once every couple of weeks? Because she couldn't afford them."

"How did she afford the country club fees, then?" Michelle asked.

"For the last three years Judge Sutherland paid them for her. He died last spring, but there was mention of his gifts in the correspondence grandmother kept—a favor to an old friend, he termed it."

"Nothing?" Abby repeated.

Caroline pulled the thick envelope from her tote and pulled out the pages the attorney had given her. She laid them on the table for the others to read if they wanted.

"If we can sell the house for what we're asking, we'll be able to pay off the mortgage, with hopefully enough left over for taxes. If we sell the furnishings, that'll help pay her last bills. But we'll have to sell everything right away, no holding back any pieces in hopes to find a better price down the road. Selling her jewelry will get us a bit of ready cash, but the two necklaces we thought were diamonds are paste— very nice copies, but she apparently sold the originals years ago."

"Was that why she was so adamant we marry money?" Abby said slowly.

"No, she always wanted that," Michelle said. "I

remember even as a little girl her admonishing me to mind my manners so I could fit in with a certain family."

Caroline took a deep breath. "There's more."

Michelle looked at her. "Can't be worse, this has been enough of a shock."

"It doesn't have to do with money. It's about our father."

Abby and Michelle looked blank.

"Let me guess, he wasn't really married to our mother," Michelle said wryly.

"Actually, he was. Sam Williams."

"Huh?" Abby asked.

"Didn't you ever wonder why our name was Talmadge, same as grandmother's?"

"Yes, but I'm with Michelle, I thought maybe when he cut out Mother she found the marriage was bigamous or something and took back her maiden name. Or kept it all along."

"I don't think women did that as much back then. No, I think grandmother insisted. Just like she did when I left Brandon. She very much wanted me to get a divorce, you know. To marry a man fitting the Talmadge name. She was obsessed with the Talmadge name."

"So Sam Williams is dear old daddy," Michelle said scathingly.

"I don't think he left voluntarily," Caroline said slowly.

The waitress set their plates on the table, asking if they needed anything else. When she departed, both Abby and Michelle ignored their meal.

"More," Abby said.

"I should have told you earlier, but I wanted to make sure. Eugenia rambled those last few days before she died. Said all sorts of things. The worst of which was that she had sent Sam packing."

"Delusional," Abby said. "I've seen it all the time in the hospital. Doesn't mean anything."

"Maybe not, but added to what else I found, I think it does."

Caroline related how Eugenia had kept Brandon and her apart. Then she showed them the letter from Edith. Finally she repeated as best she could remember her grandmother's exact words.

Stunned, the sisters looked at each other.

"Wow," Michelle said.

"Amen!" said Abby.

"She was a witch!" Michelle said. "It's unconscionable what she did to you and Brandon. I remember how you were hurting when you lost the baby and how devastated you felt when Brandon never called. So now it turns out he did try. Many times. I'd like to wring her neck!"

Caroline nodded. "You can't imagine the rage I felt when I learned about it. And about our father, too."

She looked down at her salad, pushing it around the plate with her fork. "I always thought I'd done something to make him leave."

"That's dumb—and you know it!" Michelle said. "You were a little girl. He was a grown man."

Caroline shrugged. "I'm telling you what I thought. I think it made it easier for Eugenia to drive a wedge between

Brandon and me. I guess I sort of expected him to desert me like our father had done earlier."

"Now what? Is he alive?"

Caroline shrugged. "I have no idea."

"I'd like to know. If he's alive, I'd want to ask him why he left," Michelle said slowly. "And why he never came back for us. Do you suppose he didn't hear about Mama's death? Maybe he thinks we're all living happy lives with her. How could he stay away from his own children? Surely over the years he'd have found some way to contact us."

"It had to be something grandmother did. Once I discover the full story, I guess I'd want to see if we can find him. To get answers. Maybe learn what he's been doing all this time. Find out if he ever missed us," Caroline said. "But right now, I'd settle for learning the full story."

The sisters were silent for a long time. Abby nibbled on her lunch. Michelle drew patterns on the condensation of her glass of iced tea as she leafed through the packet the attorney had provided.

"What next?" she asked after a long moment.

Caroline shook her head. "I don't know. That's why I wanted to get together. We have to decide how to handle the estate."

"According to the expenses the lawyer totaled, the estate owes a lot of money."

Abby looked at her shrewdly. "I bet Brandon would help."

"I'm not asking," Caroline said firmly.

"Why not?" Michelle asked. "He's loaded, if what I hear

about him is anything to go by. And I bet he wouldn't mind—especially if you two are getting back together."

"Oh, right—and have him think that I want to be together for what he can do monetarily?"

"He's not going to think that. The man was crazy about you. He must still be to want you back after all this time." Michelle said. "Ask him."

"No. And I don't need you to tell me what happened five years ago. Do you think I've stopped thinking about it for a single day?"

"Then sell the stuff and get as much as you can for everything right away and we'll see if it'll cover the bills," Abby interjected.

"We could have an estate sale, I suppose," Caroline said, thinking aloud.

Abby laughed, the sound infectious. Michelle smiled.

"What?" Caroline asked.

"Won't grandmother spin in her grave to know her snooty family was reduced to an estate sale to make ends meet?"

Caroline smiled.

"That's settled then. Tell us what you want us to do. I'll ask for whatever weekend off if that's when you'll have the estate sale. I want to hear more about Brandon," Abby said.

It was late afternoon by the time Michelle dropped Caroline at Brandon's condo. She and Abby promised to go to Baton Rouge the next weekend to do what they could to speed up the process of winding up Eugenia's life.

Caroline had already contacted a real estate agent to list

Talmadge Hall, and would contact an auction house to arrange sale of the furnishings. The appraisers were due to finish the next week, so they'd then have an idea of the taxes needed and the total of the bills the attorney was compiling.

On the way back to Brandon's place, Caroline had Michelle stop at the grocery store. She planned to make Shrimp Creole for dinner, one of Brandon's favorite meals. Buying all the ingredients, she hesitated buying cooking utensils. Even though he'd said he didn't cook much, surely he had the pots and pans.

"Are you going to be okay?" Michelle asked, as she pulled into a parking space near Brandon's building.

Caroline nodded. "I'm still reeling as I realize the lengths our grandmother went to get her own way. And to keep up appearances. But I'll get through it all. Do you think anyone cared but her? I mean, she could have cut back on expenses, lived a quieter life."

"After all I heard today, I have no idea how her mind worked. I can't believe what you told us about our father. Sell the place, make up with Brandon and let's get on with our lives," Michelle said.

Brandon wasn't home when Caroline let herself in. She experienced a moment of disappointment, but shook it off. He hadn't known when she was expected back. He'd be along when he finished his meeting.

Busying herself in the kitchen, Caroline forgot the cares of the estate and took pleasure in the simple task of cooking. She'd loved experimenting with new recipes when they'd been married, relished taking care of her husband. It had been a long time, but her contentment increased as the afternoon wore on.

When the Shrimp Creole was simmering, she began to clean up. Brandon had plenty of pans and bowls. One she recognized by the chip on the edge. They'd found it at a place near the university on one of their first weekends together. Slowly she dried the bowl, remembering how happy they'd been.

Remembering, too, the long, lonely years they'd lived apart. Tears filled her eyes.

She could never get those years back—the time she should have been at Brandon's side, helping him, encouraging him and loving him.

A sob escaped. So much time lost. So much love lost.

"Caroline?"

Brandon turned her around.

She gazed up at him, catching her lower lip between her teeth, blinking the tears from her eyes. She hadn't heard him come in.

"What is it?" His thumbs brushed her lashes, brushing away the tears. "Did you hurt yourself?"

She shook her head and stepped closer, feeling like she'd come home when his arms drew her into his embrace.

"I missed you," she said, holding on tightly.

"It's only been a few hours," he said, his hands soothing as they rubbed across her back.

She shook her head, leaning into him.

"I mean the last five years. I needed you and turned away. You needed me and I wasn't there."

She tried to stem the tears, but they wouldn't stop despite her efforts. "I'd give anything to turn back the clock."

"I know, sweetheart. Now that I know more, I'd have done things differently. But the past can't be undone. We can only go forward."

She took a deep breath. Decision time.

"Let's go forward—together. I don't think I can bear to be apart another five years," she said, holding him as if she'd never let him go.

"That's what we'll do, then," he said.

He kissed her again and Caroline gave back every speck of love in her. She wanted to be with him, share his life, learn what was important to him these days and what he couldn't abide.

She was breathless when he pulled back and gazed into her eyes. Suddenly he smiled, swung her up in his arms and carried her to his bedroom. Setting her on her feet beside the large bed, he looked her frankly in the face.

"No turning back, now, Caroline. We go forward together right? Us against the world no matter what."

She nodded "No matter what!"

She loved him so much!

"Together."

It was only as she dished up the Shrimp Creole some time later that Caroline realized Brandon had not spoken a single word of love.

To be fair, she hadn't said anything, either.

But he had to love her, didn't he? He wouldn't want to have a marriage without love.

Later Brandon stared out across the river. Night had fallen. In the background he could hear Caroline rinsing their dishes. Dinner had been wonderful—one of his favorite meals. When they'd been together before, she'd made it as a special celebration. Was she celebrating?

He should be. But something nagged him. He'd been concerned when he found her crying this afternoon. The gut-wrenching feeling reminiscent of when she'd cried so much after losing the baby.

The small rituals of domesticity with her fixing dinner warmed him. He'd been alone too long. Could they make it last this time?

There was something still not right.

Taking a sip of the cognac in his glass, he realized what it was. Never once had she mentioned the word love.

If she didn't love him, why did she want to resume their marriage?

Had he made a mistake telling her his reason for a divorce? Was she influenced by the thought of the money she'd be entitled to if his company became as large and successful as analysts predicted?

He didn't want to believe that, but it nagged him all the same.

Chapter Ten

Caroline hated to leave New Orleans Sunday night. Brandon asked her to stay longer, but she had too much to do to let herself be talked into staying.

"The sooner I get things wrapped up in Baton Rouge, the better," she explained. There were still a million things to decide. She wanted some time without distractions to do that. Then she'd have to face closing things up in Dallas.

"I'll come up on Wednesday," he said, kissing her gently.

"I'd like that," she said shyly.

Not wanting to cling, almost afraid to let go, she hugged him tightly.

"I'll count the minutes until then," she whispered in his ear.

She was almost afraid of the newfound happiness. For so long, she'd thought her life would stretch out forever alone and lonely. Now they were being given a second chance. It was almost too wonderful to trust.

"Drive carefully," he said gruffly, kissing her long and hard.

Monday Caroline contacted an estate auction sales office and made arrangements to hold a sale within the month.

Tuesday she read the rest of the correspondence and found nothing further relating to her father. Proof apparently wasn't going to be found in Eugenia's papers.

To see the truth in black and white would have been nice, but after what Eugenia had done between her and Brandon, she knew without further proof that her grandmother had been instrumental in driving away her father. She didn't know how, or why, but she no longer needed the proof she'd once longed for.

"More mail came since you were here last," Rosalie said when Caroline sat down for dinner. The older woman plopped a stack of envelopes, fliers and catalogs down beside Caroline's place.

"Eat first before reading."

Caroline nodded and waited until Rosalie had returned to the kitchen. Slowly, while eating, she sifted through the mail. Not much worth even looking at. She received some of the same catalogs at her place.

There was a letter with shaky writing addressed to Eugenia Talmadge's Granddaughters.

Intrigued, Caroline opened it. A sympathy card. From Edith Strong! She was sorry to hear of Eugenia's death. They'd been friends as young women. Her sympathy was with her granddaughters.

She stared at it, a strange premonition taking hold. Was this the same Edith of the letter?

Looking at the return address, Caroline noted it was an assisted living home in Baton Rouge.

Not waiting to finish her meal, she dashed to her purse

to dig out her phone.

"Madison," Brandon's deep voice immediately answered.

"Hi, it's Caroline. Guess what I just got?"

"A winning lottery ticket worth ten million dollars if the excitement in your voice is to be believed," he said.

"Better than that! Remember the letter from Edith—the one that made mention of Eugenia's interfering?"

"Yes."

"I think I have a card from that same Edith—a sympathy card to her granddaughters on the loss of our grandmother. Brandon—she's living in a retirement home not too far from here."

"And you want to go see her," he guessed.

She laughed, giddy with excitement. "Yes! Maybe she can tell me what I need to know."

"Tomorrow, we'll go tomorrow when I get there. Wait for me. I'll arrive around one, all right?"

Caroline didn't want to wait another minute, but she knew a few more hours wouldn't matter—not after all this time. And she'd like to have Brandon with her.

"Okay, I'll wait. But don't be late."

"I won't. I want to see you," he said in a low tone.

She leaned against the wall and closed her eyes against the longing that filled her. "I want to see you, too. Yesterday and today seemed endless!"

"Tomorrow, then."

"Keep safe."

She ended the call and stashed her phone back in her purse.

He'd be here tomorrow!

Edith was almost forgotten as Caroline anticipated Brandon's arrival. She'd missed him. More these last couple of days than in the last five years, she believed.

The weekend had proved to her that they belonged together. And she was willing to take him on whatever terms he dictated. If he didn't love her anymore, it was her own fault. She loved him enough for both of them.

And talking on the phone wasn't enough. She wanted to be with him!

Grateful the baby issue had been shelved, she didn't plan to bring it up again. They'd be happy the two of them, without a baby. It wasn't the life they'd originally planned, but it'd work. She'd do her best to make it work.

Wednesday, Caroline rose, excitement and a hint of trepidation churning. She needed something to soothe her overwrought nerves, not exacerbate them. Brandon would be in Baton Rouge soon, only a few more hours! She could hardly wait. First she'd see him, and then they may find out the answers she'd been searching for.

Eating dry toast and some tea, she hurried through breakfast and began going through yet another bedroom as if plunging into work would bring one o'clock that much faster.

Brandon didn't arrive until after one. She'd been checking the drive every couple of minutes, anticipation growing with each second..

Caroline grabbed her purse and almost ran the short distance to greet him.

"Hi," she said breathlessly.

"Hi yourself," He leaned over to kiss her.

"Hmm," she said, giving in to the kiss. "I've missed you. It was awful to be apart, but the getting back together isn't bad," she murmured.

"Let's go find your grandmother's friend."

Caroline was all for that. The sooner the task was completed, the sooner they could be alone.

She took the sympathy card and envelope with her.

"I hope she remembers," Caroline said, as they settled in Brandon's car. "Sometimes people in homes like that have dementia. What if she doesn't remember?"

"Then you're no worse off than you are right now," he said practically.

The drive to the retirement home was short. Before long they parked adjacent to the beautiful grounds of Sunny Acres. Walking up the wide sidewalk, Caroline felt almost sick with tension. She swallowed hard, hoping she'd find the end to the puzzle here.

If not, would she give up her quest? Was it too late to find her father, learn from him what had happened.

Her mother and father never had the opportunity to get back together. She felt sad thinking of how badly her grandmother had interfered with other peoples' lives.

They were shown in to a bright parlor and in only a few minutes an older lady arrived using a walker.

"Edith Strong?" Caroline asked, standing and crossing to the elderly woman, offering her hand.

"Yes. I don't get visitors very often. Who are you?"

She looked older than Eugenia had, her hair entirely white, wispy and thin. Her eyes peered up at Caroline through thick glasses.

"I'm Caroline Talmadge—Eugenia Talmadge's granddaughter. One of them. I received your card yesterday."

Edith shook her hand and motioned for Caroline to sit on the nearby chair. She slowly sat in a straight back chair as Caroline introduced Brandon.

"I thought for sure I'd go before Eugenia. I fell and broke my hip four years ago. I won't ever walk unaided, you know. Most old folks like me don't get up and about after something like that. But Eugenia—she had so daggum much determination that I thought she'd outlive us all." She shook her head again.

"You and she were friends," Caroline said, sitting on the edge of the chair. Impatiently she wanted to find out everything but she kept her voice calm. Brandon leaned against the wall a few steps away, quietly observing. She flicked him a glance and then looked back at Edith.

"We were good friends for a long time when we were young." Her expression became pensive. "Weathered a lot of ups and downs, I can tell you."

"Was one of the downs when she drove my father away?" Caroline asked gently.

Edith looked at her sharply. "Know about that, do you?"

Caroline nodded. "Not the details, though. Could you fill those in?"

Edith gazed off into the distance for a minute, then sighed softly and began to speak.

"I told her at the time she was a fool to do it. It isn't right that a person play God that away. And once her Amanda died, I think she regretted what she'd done. Amanda'd be alive today, I believe, if Eugenia hadn't interfered. But her pride was something awful and her determination to get what she wanted. The only time I've seen her so furious was when Amanda came home after marrying Sam Williams."

"My parents were married a number of years and had children together. How could Eugenia have driven my father away?" Caroline asked.

"Amanda married him in New Orleans. He was an oil wildcatter—worked the rigs in the gulf. They had you almost before Eugenia knew they'd been married. I suspected Amanda wasn't chancing anything going wrong. She didn't want to do anything but be married to Sam. He was a fine figure of a man—tall, broad shouldered. Dark hair."

She studied Caroline for a moment. "You look of him, a bit. And he sure adored you. Many's the time I was at Eugenia's when your father tossed you up in the air laughing with you, claiming you were his sunshine."

Caroline swallowed hard. Her father had loved her! She blinked back tears.

"What happened?"

"Tom Prescott's what happened," Edith snapped.

"Who's Tom Prescott?" Caroline recognized the name— the Prescotts were an old Louisiana family—with a fortune from cotton and rice.

"He was a young man who became smitten with your

mother. And he came from the kind of background Eugenia wanted for Amanda—old family, old money. Not some jumped up, no-account wildcatter." Edith peered at Caroline.

"Eugenia did all she could to throw Tom and Amanda together—to no avail, Amanda had eyes only for her Sam. So Eugenia trumped up charges against your father for the murder of an old man. Got old Judge Sutherland to help her. He'd wanted to marry your grandmother for years. She didn't want to give up the Talmadge name, but wasn't above using his devotion when it suited her."

"They accused my father of murder?" Caroline was stunned.

"Eugenia met with Sam privately—swore she had proof that would convict him, and that she'd use it if he didn't leave. Had the judge issue a warrant and everything. Quiet like, though. She didn't want her name dragged in the mud. I don't know what that proof was, but it must have been pretty strong. Sam left to protect his family and Amanda soon died of a broken heart. She was pregnant with that third girl, what's her name?"

"Abigail, Abby."

"Abby. That's right. I don't think Sam even knew there was another one on the way. He lit out and we never heard from him again. Of course your mother died soon after Abby was born. I don't know if he heard about her passing or not, but if he did, maybe he felt there was no reason to return. Eugenia still held all the cards. And there's no statue of limitations on murder."

Her eyes shifted as if she gazed into the distant past.

"They were a fine young couple, so in love, so happy. Eugenia couldn't stand that, you know. She wanted her Amanda allied with the Prescotts. Instead, her girl died young. Eugenia never said another word about Sam. But I sure have wondered over the years if she ever regretted what she'd done."

"There were reasons to return, his daughters!" Caroline said.

"Honey, he knew that harridan of a grandmother of yours would slap him in jail so fast it'd make your head spin. He didn't have the money or resources to fight a Talmadge. Or a murder charge."

Caroline shook her head. "There must have been something he could have done."

"I told Eugenia she'd done a terrible thing. But she wanted that Tom Prescott for Amanda and wouldn't be stopped."

"Instead Mama died," Caroline said softly.

"She sure did. I always thought it was from a broken heart. She had no idea what her mother had done. That was a sad day. And it knocked Eugenia for a loop. But she rallied and said she'd have three chances now to do the Talmadges proud. She had three granddaughters."

"None of us married to suit her, either." She glanced at Brandon. "But not for lack of trying on her part. Wouldn't you have thought she'd learn from what happened with her daughter? She pulled almost the same stunt between my husband and me."

"No, child. I surely wouldn't expect she'd learn from the

past. She was one determined woman. What Eugenia wanted, Eugenia did all she could to get it—by fair means or foul. I wrote her once about it—she was never the same friend afterward. Our friendship dwindled. But I was truly sorry when I heard of her death a few days ago. We were girls together, you know. Don't have many friends left who remember when we were girls," Edith said.

Brandon didn't say anything as he walked beside Caroline to the car. He tried to imagine how she felt. He was furious with Eugenia, not only for the separation she fostered between him and Caroline, but for the three little girls who had been denied a father's love and support during their growing years. All for her own idea of what her daughter's life should be.

"Are you all right?" he asked as she stopped by the car door.

She nodded and looked up at him.

"I'm sad for my parents. They got a raw deal. But my father didn't desert us! He was driven away. A murder charge would be enough to drive anyone away and keep him away. Especially from a rich and powerful family like the Talmadges. I wonder what happened to the warrant? Is there still one out for my father?"

"We can check in with the local police and find out." He lightly touched her shoulder. "I'm glad you let me come with you."

She nodded. "I almost didn't, I was so impatient this morning, but figured I might need the moral support."

"And I can give you that?"

"That and a lot more," she said, reaching up to brush her lips across his cheek. "I can't wait to call Abby and Michelle and let them know."

"What next?"

"Home, I guess. Unless you want to stop at the police station first?"

"Might as well get it all cleared up this afternoon. Are you going to pursue this?"

"Pursue what?" she asked.

"Finding your father."

"I guess so. I hadn't thought that far ahead. Actually just finding out the truth is a lot to deal with. Though I guess it's important to find him. To learn what he's done over the years. And let him know his daughters are doing all right."

The stop at the police station turned up no outstanding warrants for a Sam Williams. There was no indication that one had ever been issued. There was no way to tell if Eugenia's threat had been an empty one or if Judge Sutherland had rescinded it long ago.

On a hunch, Brandon drove to the library. Looking through back issues of the local paper, they found an article concerning a death of an old itinerant laborer. And another one several months later that announced the killer had been apprehended. The date of that paper was shortly after Amanda's death.

Caroline made copies of both articles before turning off the microfilm reader.

"It's so sad," she said softly, looking at Brandon. "I wonder if my mother ever found out why Sam left? If she ever heard from him again. I know how devastated she must have been."

She reached out and touched his hand. "And history almost repeated itself with us, didn't it?"

He turned his hand, taking hers and bringing it to his lips to kiss her palm. "Almost. Eugenia was a dangerous woman!"

"Ready to go back home?" he asked as they left the library.

"Yes. Rosalie knew you were coming and is preparing another elaborate dinner for us."

"Sounds good."

"Just don't get used to such fancy meals. I won't have as much time to spend on cooking while I'm trying to get going in real estate in New Orleans."

"About that. I've been thinking," he said. "Real estate isn't exactly like office work. You have to know the area, neighborhoods, school districts, shopping areas, and a lot more when trying to match people to the perfect home."

She nodded. She'd spent most of the last five years learning all she could in and around Dallas and Fort Worth.

"Whereas I can pretty much work anywhere."

He saw her turn to stare at him.

"What are you saying?" she asked.

"Nothing says we have to live in New Orleans. I can fly over a few times a month if I'm needed in the office. In the meantime, set up a branch in Dallas. The company is poised to expand, I'll just expand in Texas."

"That would be wonderful!" she exclaimed.

If he hadn't been driving, she'd have throw her arms around him and kissed him. The possibilities exploded.

Brandon's cell phone rang just as they arrived at Talmadge Hall. He answered as Caroline indicated she'd go on inside.

As she hurried up the stairs, she tried to take in everything she' d learned today. From her grandmother's egregious behavior to Brandon's being willing to move to Dallas.

Hurrying up the stairs, she wanted to change into something more comfortable than her suit. She wouldn't mind taking a brief nap, she felt tired and drained. Learning the history of her parents' brief marriage and its ending had been almost more than she could stand. She needed to call her sisters. They'd be blown away. Lying down, she closed her eyes. She'd rest just for a moment and then call Michelle and Abby.

"Miss Caroline, dinner's ready," Rosalie said, leaning over her and shaking her shoulder gently.

Caroline opened her eyes. Instead of resting for a minute, she'd fallen sound asleep!

"And you best look to finding Mr. Brandon. He was wandering around the downstairs rooms for a while. I saw him in the study. But now I don't know where he is. I don't want dinner to get cold!"

Caroline quickly brushed her hair then ran down the steps. She peeked into every room on the ground floor, but didn't find Brandon.

Going out on the veranda, she looked around the yard.

There he was walking on the levee.

She called to Rosalie that she'd be right back and started off to intercept him.

Smiling happily, she didn't realize at first he didn't reciprocate.

"Hi," she said as she drew close. Her eyes searched his face. He looked tired. An early night for them would be good.

Brandon said nothing, just looked at her, his face impassive.

Oh-oh, Caroline thought, now what?

Her heart began to beat heavily. Had he received bad news?

"Rosalie has dinner ready," she said brightly.

"I won't be staying for dinner."

"What's wrong?" The smile faded.

His gaze was hard, direct.

"You tell me, Caroline." He stepped closer and gripped her arms. "When did you plan to tell me about your grandmother's debts?"

Caroline stared at him. Her heart raced. Heat washed through her.

"I don't know that I ever was," she said slowly. "It doesn't concern you, just my sisters and me."

"Didn't you think I'd find it interesting that you decided to restart this marriage at exactly the time I'm poised to make a huge profit while your own personal fortune has vanished?"

"You think I wanted to come back because of money?"

she asked, hurt he'd ever suspect her of such a thing.

Yet hadn't she withheld the information for that very fear?

"You're good with that disingenuous display of amazement."

His words hurt.

"When did you find out?" he asked sharply.

She hesitated, then raised her chin. "Two weeks ago. Eugenia's attorney called me in to his office to go over the estate. That's the reason I met with my sisters when I was in New Orleans. It impacts them too. And me. But not you."

She broke his hold and stepped back. "How did you find out?"

"Your attorney called this afternoon. When you didn't respond to Rosalie's call, I took it."

"You should have taken a message."

"The timing of this reconciliation seems mighty convenient to me, don't you think? I foolishly try to establish a base of honesty by telling you about the company's expansion plans. You still held me off, but once you learn of your grandmother's lack of money, suddenly you want to move back. Suddenly, it's a good idea to start over."

Caroline felt sick. He interpreted everything wrong. Her grandmother's estate, or lack of one, had nothing to do with her wanting to start over with Brandon. Hadn't he felt any of the attraction she felt?

She loved him, hadn't he felt even a glimmer of that?

Did he feel anything for her? He'd never said a word about love or caring.

"If that's what you believe," she said tightly, "please leave."

"Want to explain the timing if nothing else?"

She tightened her lips and shook her head. The last thing she'd do is argue.

The hurt pierced as sharp as last time.

She'd thought they'd been given a second chance. Now she knew she'd been fooling herself.

There were no second chances.

For once her grandmother had been correct. She should have divorced the man and gotten on with her life years ago.

"I don't have to justify my actions to you. If you can't take my word that money has nothing to do with us, then I think we are better off apart."

Sweep me into your arms, tell me you love me, that money doesn't matter at all, she silently urged him.

But Brandon made no move to touch her.

Without another word, he walked away.

She remained on the levee until she heard his car leave. Slowly walking back to the house, she told Rosalie she wasn't hungry and went up to her room.

Caroline went to bed but lay awake staring at the darkness for hours. Her nap had robbed her of the fatigue she needed to sleep.

Brandon's parting words echoed over and over in her mind, keeping her restless and awake. How could he have thought that about her? How could he think she only wanted his money? If that was the way he thought, she was better off going it alone.

The next day Caroline collected all the papers she needed from Eugenia's desk. She walked through the house one last time and marked the items each of her sisters and herself had decided to keep.

She gave Rosalie instructions on keeping the house dusted and aired out each day until the estate sale, then left. She had no intention of returning until the day of the sale. And maybe not even then, if one of her sisters could handle it.

Refusing to think about Brandon, she headed for the airport.

By the time she reached her condo her lack of sleep was catching up with her, as was her refusal to eat. She felt queasy and tired, disheartened. Falling into bed, she was grateful for the sleep that overtook her.

Saturday Caroline slept in late. Feeling refreshed when she woke, she realized she'd forgotten to let her sisters know what she'd found out from Edith. She called Michelle and told her she was no longer at Talmadge Hall. She also told her about meeting with Edith and asked her to call Abby.

"Things okay, Caroline?" Michelle asked.

"Sure, what's not to be okay?" Caroline tried flippantly. But she mustn't have been successful.

"I don't know, but you sound upset. Did something happen in Dallas that you had to return so soon?"

"I guess I'm upset to find out our father was driven away by the machinations of a manipulative old woman? And Edith thought our mother died of a broken heart! We were robbed of both of our parents!"

"It was the flu," Michelle said. "Grandmother told us that often enough."

"But if a person has no will to live, they give in to illnesses that would not ordinarily affect them."

"Now you sound like Abby."

"You don't have to be a nurse to know that."

"So what's next?"

"The estate sale will be within the month. I marked the furniture we each wanted. The appraisers are finished. The tax bill will be forthcoming soon, I'm sure. I think I have a full recount of the medical—"

"Caroline, what's up with you and Brandon? Will you be there to handle all that or be living here by then?"

Caroline swallowed desperately and tried for control. She refused to let that man get to her a second time. Taking a shaky breath, she tried to keep her voice even.

"Brandon and I are not resuming our marriage after all."

"What?"

Quickly explaining what happened before getting off the phone, Caroline was surprised at how much she hurt.

Better get used to it, girl, she admonished herself.

She'd done it once before, she could do it again. Work would be the best antidote. She understood more and more why Brandon had found solace in work after she'd lost the baby.

Thursday she received a letter from Brandon's attorneys with the divorce papers that Rosalie had forwarded to her.

Angry at the callous way he proceeded, she fumed all afternoon.

She ought to teach him a lesson. She wasn't the money hungry gold-digger he thought, but maybe she should give him a taste of that. Maybe she'd show the man she wasn't easily pushed aside.

The following week a registered letter arrived—another letter from Brandon's attorneys and a new set of divorce papers.

Caroline began to make plans.

By Friday afternoon her head was reeling. She'd had enough. Tomorrow morning, early, she was heading for New Orleans to see Brandon. To finalize things once and for all.

Early the next morning Caroline parked her rental car across the street from Brandon's apartment building, considering it a good omen to get an early flight and then find a parking place so easily. At the lobby door, she started to ring the downstairs bell. Then hesitated. Rummaging in her purse, she found the key he'd given her. Opening the heavy glass door, she sailed up to his apartment without a qualm. The next few minutes would determine her life once and for all.

Odd how she felt calm and controlled. She should be ranting and raving or scared to death.

Maybe that would all come later.

But for now, she wasn't some young twenty-year-old anymore. Her grandmother was no longer in the picture. For better or worse, she was on her own now. It could be that some of Eugenia's determination had shown up in her oldest granddaughter.

She opened his apartment and stepped inside, listening.

The aroma of fresh coffee filled the air. She heard the rustle of a newspaper from the kitchen. He was probably eating breakfast. She glanced at her watch—at 9:34 in the morning. He should have been at work hours ago, never mind that it was Saturday. She'd planned to stop here first and then check at his office.

Slowly she walked to the kitchen door and stopped, the sight of him unexpectedly surprising her. He looked tired—lines bracketed his mouth that hadn't been there a few days ago. He hadn't shaved. The sweats he wore were baggy and old. The man was worth a ton of money and still wore old baggy sweats from five years ago?

Though she didn't move or make a sound, he looked up suddenly and froze. Slowly, he lowered the paper.

Boldly, Caroline raised her chin and crossed the room. "I have two things to say to you. Depending on how you react, we will end this foolishness one way or the other."

"What foolishness?"

Even his voice had a disturbing effect on her nerves. Her knees felt wobbly, but she refused to sit down. Standing gave her the power position.

Opening her purse, she drew out the divorce papers—and the additional sheet her attorney had prepared.

"I will tell you this only once. You can accept it or not. If not, then I will sign the papers you so kindly sent—with this one additional one that says you relinquish everything that is mine. I want nothing from you, Brandon, and I expect you to sign this sheet relinquishing anything of mine of which I now possess."

His eyes narrowed as he studied her. "Go on."

She took a deep breath—now or never!

"I love you," she said baldly. "I realize that I haven't told you that in five years. I don't know how you feel, but I wanted you to know that I love you. I have from almost the first day we met. I probably will until the day I die. I agreed to resume our marriage for the sole reason that I love you. I wanted to be with you. We were young when tragedy hit and we didn't know how to cope. I've learned coping techniques over the years but that changes nothing. I still feel as strongly about you as ever. I never asked for a divorce, never dated other men, never wanted anyone but you in all my life."

"And our baby."

She nodded. "That goes without saying." She took a deep breath. "Whether you believe me or not is up to you. But it was never about money. Not for me."

Slowly he rose, took a step that placed him right in front of her.

The back of his fingers brushed against her cheek, the hard glint in his eye belying the gentleness of his touch. "And if I say I don't believe you?"

Chapter Eleven

"Then I'll sign the papers here and now, as long as you agree to the additional term that my attorney prepared," she said evenly.

Brandon tried to ignore the surge of feelings that filled him with her declaration of love. He'd never loved anyone as intensely, as completely as he did Caroline Talmadge.

He'd been so long without her, he actually thought he could live the rest of his life and never see her again.

These last few weeks proved him wrong. He'd missed her with a longing that scared him. She was right. They'd been young when they'd first married and he'd been bent on proving to himself and to the world he could succeed. But at what cost?

He didn't want to be alone—he wanted Caroline in his life.

Did she really love him? Looking into her eyes convinced him—if he'd ever truly doubted it.

Despite the interference of her grandmother, despite the years apart, despite the misunderstanding and evidence to the contrary, and his cynical lawyer's remarks, he believed her.

Slowly, he cupped her face. "I love you, Caroline."

She released her breath in a whoosh and clung to his wrists.

"I was bluffing," she confessed. "I don't think I could have walked away no matter what you said."

"Good bluff."

He lowered his head and kissed her, drawing her tightly into his arms where she belonged. The feel of her body set his afire. Her scent sparked memories and desire. Her warmth lit a conflagration and the way she returned his kiss told him he had his true love.

They'd sort the rest out later. For now he just wanted to hold her, love her.

A long time later Brandon lifted his head, taking in her flushed cheeks, the stars that seemed to shine in her eyes, the damp, slightly swollen lips that had so passionately returned his kisses.

"You said you had two things to say. Before we move into another area of the apartment, what's the second?"

Swallowing hard, she tilted her head, as if trying to judge his reaction.

"It can't be that bad," he offered. "Haven't we got the worst behind us yet?"

She shook her head. "I was afraid to come here today, but I was so angry with you, it gave me false courage." She hesitated. "But I'm even more afraid about being pregnant," she said in a rush.

The familiar pain struck. He wanted kids. He wanted to give them the love his parents had given him, but provide more for them than he'd had as a child. He wanted to spend lazy vacations at the beach or the mountains. Take them to Disneyland. Teach them to play ball and to enjoy the outdoors.

But if it wasn't to be, he could live with that. He knew Caroline had suffered terribly with the miscarriage—only now was he coming to understand the full extent. Taking a deep breath, he rested his forehead against hers.

"Then we won't get pregnant," he said slowly, relinquishing a dream.

He wanted Caroline on whatever terms she stated.

"Oh, Brandon!" She laughed up at him even as tears welled in her eyes. "That's so sweet, but a little late. I am pregnant."

"What?" Shock coursed through him.

She nodded, the tears brimming over. "I had it confirmed yesterday." She blushed slightly. "I think we must have forgotten to take precautions at least once. But I'm still scared to death. My doctor said it should be all right, but what if it isn't? I don't think I could bear it."

"You're pregnant?"

She nodded, smiling despite the tears, which he tried to brush away.

Astonishment gave way to incredulity, then a deep abiding happiness. It was as if they were starting over, past and present merging to forge the strong future they once hoped to have.

"I'll see nothing happens to you this time, Caroline. I promise!"

"Knowing I have your love will be enough. We'll make it this time." She reached up to kiss him. Then pulled back staring into his eyes.

"What?"

He was more attuned to her than he thought. He could tell she had more to say. For a moment fear clutched him. Was there something she hadn't told him? Something serious, about her own health or the pregnancy?

"Is there something wrong? Something I need to know?"

She shook her head, her smile wobbly.

"There is something, tell me."

"Would you think me really silly to want to get married again? I mean, I know we've been married all along, but somehow, this feels like starting over. Like it's all new. I don't know, I just thought on the flight here that if we started over we could do it with a proper renewal of our vows."

"A wedding like you'd wear a white dress and veil?" He smiled, imagining her walking down the church aisle toward him.

"Hardly white and it doesn't need to be elaborate. But maybe a nice dress and hat?"

"I'd love to see you walk down the aisle to me! I'd love to renew our vows—in front of God and all our friends this time. We'll do it up right. No courthouse this time, but your church. With your sisters there and friends. My mom'll love the idea. I don't think you're being silly, sweetheart. I think it's a great plan. And it would make it twice as hard to ever separate again."

Three months later

"You look beautiful," Michelle said, fussing with the roses in Caroline's hair.

"Well, I feel like a blimp," Caroline complained, turning sideways to the mirror. The soft swell of her belly hardly extended enough to disrupt the flow of the lovely pale blue dress. The inverted pleat on the short skirt gave way enough to let the whole world know she was pregnant. She smiled despite her complaint.

"A bride isn't supposed to be almost five months' pregnant."

"No, but a wife can be." Impulsively Michelle hugged her sister. "I'm so happy for you. And look on the bright side. This time you get to be a June bride."

Caroline returned the hug, smiling broadly. "We barely made it into June. We were lucky the church was available this first weekend. I'm more thankful the morning sickness is behind me."

"It would look a little silly to have the bride interrupt the ceremony while she took a mad dash to the bathroom," Abby agreed, handing Caroline the lovely bouquet of pale pink roses Brandon had sent.

Matching corsages were already pinned to her shoulder and Michelle's.

"Half of Baton Rouge is out there, I swear," Michelle said a minute later peeking out to the church.

"Well we are Talmadges. Eugenia gave us that."

It was the same church she and her sisters had attended

all their lives. The one Eugenia had planned to have each granddaughter marry in. At least that part of the old woman's schemes was coming true.

Only she'd have thought the man wrong.

Caroline knew Eugenia was the one who'd have been wrong. Brandon was perfect. Anyone who saw them together knew that.

"It was nice of you to send a car for Edith Strong," Abby said, fussing with her own hair, giving up with a sigh.

"She's a nice woman and I'm grateful for her telling me the truth about what happened with our father."

"You never carried it any further. Want to?" Michelle asked casually.

"What do you mean?

"I mean knowing he didn't leave us of his own volition, is that enough?"

Caroline shrugged. "I had so much to do with winding up the estate long distance from Dallas, and finding a new place for me and my family." She smiled as she said that. The new house in Fort Worth was large enough for several children. And maybe a dog.

"I know he didn't abandon us, he was driven away. Nothing can change that, you know. It's made a huge difference in how I look at things. We grew up without a father, without a mother. I'd change things in a heartbeat if I could, but I can't, so I'm making sure this next generation has both parents," she said firmly, placing her hand protectively over her stomach.

"Besides, what do you suggest we do? The man's been

gone for twenty-three years, and who knows where he went? He's probably built himself a new life—and who could blame him? He could be anywhere in the world. I have a new house to decorate and a husband who's proving to be very demanding."

She smiled, not that she'd have it any other way. Brandon had taken to bringing work home and then abandoning it to spend the time with her. His workaholic ways were changing since they'd moved to Dallas. And she knew she could count on him to be with her whenever she needed him in the future.

That had been another promise.

"They're starting the wedding march," Abby said. She hugged her older sister. "Be happy!"

"How can I not help it with Brandon?"

Her sisters flanking her, Caroline started down the aisle to the man whom she'd always love.

Arriving at his side, she reached for his hand, just as she felt a flutter of life deep inside. They'd come full circle. They were stronger now and could manage whatever life threw their way—together.

Today would seal that promise.

"I love you," she whispered as the pastor took his place before them.

"I love you, Caroline, and always will," Brandon replied, leaning over to kiss her before the ceremony even began.

—The End—

Did you enjoy this story?
If so, you may enjoy the next book in
Bayou Nights series, **Michelle's Marriage Deal.**